the RACHEL RILEY Diaries

THE MEANING OF LIFE

Other books by Joanna Nadin

My So-Called Life
The Life of Riley
My (Not So) Simple Life
Back to Life
The Facts of Life

Buttercup Mash

JOANNA NADIN

the RACHEL RILEY Diaries

THE MEANING OF LIFE

OXFORD
UNIVERSITY PRESS

OXFORD

UNIVERSITY PRESS

Great Clarendon Street, Oxford OX2 6DP

Oxford University Press is a department of the University of Oxford.
It furthers the University's objective of excellence in research, scholarship,
and education by publishing worldwide in

Oxford   New York

Auckland   Cape Town   Dar es Salaam   Hong Kong   Karachi
Kuala Lumpur   Madrid   Melbourne   Mexico City   Nairobi
New Delhi   Shanghai   Taipei   Toronto

With offices in

Argentina   Austria   Brazil   Chile   Czech Republic   France   Greece
Guatemala   Hungary   Italy   Japan   Poland   Portugal   Singapore
South Korea   Switzerland   Thailand   Turkey   Ukraine   Vietnam

Oxford is a registered trade mark of Oxford University Press
in the UK and in certain other countries

British Library Cataloguing in Publication Data
Data available

ISBN: 987-0-19-273386-3
1 3 5 7 9 10 8 6 4 2

Printed in Great Britain

Paper used in the production of this book is a natural,
recyclable product made from wood grown in sustainable forests.
The manufacturing process conforms to the environmental
regulations of the country of origin.

For Millie,
My Meaning of Life

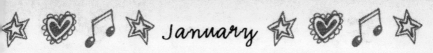
Monday 1
New Year's Day

10 a.m.

It is official. I am going out with Year Twelve sex god and part-time meat mincer Justin Statham. It is after our New Year's Eve midnight snog in Scarlet's wardrobe. I am utterly jubilant because I have spent two years trying to be his girlfriend and he is finally totally in love with me. And, most importantly, he is the ONE, despite him having small nipples (which is why Sophie Microwave Muffins Jacobs will not go out with him any more, she prefers Mr Vaughan's supersize ones, which would be fine except he is our French teacher and his nipples, fat or otherwise, should be out of bounds). For a minute, due to wardrobe blackout situation, I thought I might be snogging Jack. And was sort of hoping it was. But that was obviously just a mental lapse as Jack is Scarlet's brother. And we have far too much in common, i.e. our radical political convictions and love of tragic literature and Waitrose hummus etc. Whereas Justin and I have nothing in common and so it will be love across a divide, like Jane Eyre and Mr Rochester, or the time Fat Kylie snogged Henry Hunter-Gammon (teeth like horse, enormous bank account, very small thingy (allegedly)). We will argue about all sorts of things. If I went out with Jack we would end up on the sofa watching *Casualty* and eating HobNobs every Saturday like Mum and Dad. Although I do not think Mum and Dad will be doing any hobnobbing

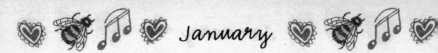

any time soon. They are still not speaking after last night's hoo-ha with Mum's ex-driving instructor Mike Wandering Hands Majors and Tuesday's ex-alcoholic mum Edie who is seemingly in love with Dad. She is mental. He is called Colin and wears vests. Which is why he and Mum (Janet, also vest-wearing) are ideally suited. Anyway, cannot go out with Jack as he is not talking to me now after he opened wardrobe door to find Justin with his tongue in my mouth and his hand hovering dangerously close to my bra strap. Scarlet is not too happy either. It is because Justin is not a goth, wears Gap, and mops up meat blood on a Saturday, and she is a strict vegetarian. That is why she is going out with John Major High head goth Trevor Pledger, who has rats and a floor-length leather coat. Although that might not last now she is giving up her hardline bat tendencies and going more EMO, so that she can wear skinny jeans. At least second-best friend Sad Ed understands me. It is because he is in a total love-across-the-divide relationship with Tuesday, i.e. her dad is gay and American and her mum is a drunkard, whereas his parents are in the Aled Jones Fan Club. Also Tuesday has tattoos and Sad Ed just has a birthmark shaped like Gary Lineker's head. It is on his left buttock. I have seen it.

10.30 a.m.
Why hasn't Justin rung? We have not seen each other for almost eight hours. Will check mobile phone again in case it is on silent by mistake and have missed crucial message of love.

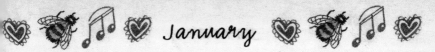

10.35 a.m.

Did miss message but was not from Justin, was from Scarlet saying when is someone coming to fetch Dad as Edna (the non-Filipina, Labour-friendly cleaner) wants to hoover up canapé crumbs and he is sprawled inconveniently on the shagpile rug. Will tell Mum.

10.45 a.m.

Mum is refusing to get Dad. James has gone instead with the dog. I feel sorry for Dad. James is more menacing than Mum when it comes to being thin-lipped and pedantic. I would go but am far too busy worrying about love life. Where, oh where, is Justin? Will check phone again. He might have called while I was downstairs.

11.00 a.m.
No messages.

11.30 a.m.
No messages.

12 noon
Still no messages. Dad is home, but has been sent to Coventry (i.e. the bedroom). Mum says he is not allowed out until he has thought about what he did last night and apologized. Dad says he cannot remember what he did last night due to uncharacteristic excessive intake of Suzy's life-threatening punch. Mum says that is the point.

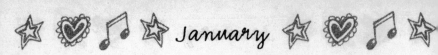

Mum is in no position to lecture Dad. She got a lift home with Mike Wandering Hands due to her uncharacteristic excessive intake (i.e. two glasses) of sherry. James says he is thinking of calling Childline.

1 p.m.

No messages. Dad is still in the bedroom. Have taken him a cheese and pickle sandwich and some Alka Seltzer. James says he should say sorry for everything, including the time he tried to hoover up spilt tea and broke the Dyson, and offer to descale the iron every month as penance. He is unusually well-versed in the ways of women (or Mum, at least) for a nine year old.

2 p.m.

Dad has apologized using James's method. He and Mum are now on the sofa looking at the John Lewis sale catalogue. But there is still an air of frostiness lingering over the pictures of polycotton duvet sets. I predict the Mum, Dad, Edie, Mr Wandering Hands love square is not over yet.

3 p.m.

No messages. Maybe it is all over and Justin was just using me in a bid to win back Sophie Microwave Muffins Jacobs from the clutches of possible pervert-in-school Mr Big Nipples Vaughan. I am just a pawn in his giant game of love chess. Oh God, will have to spend another

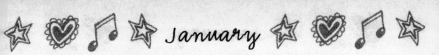
entire year being single or snogging underage rat boy Kyle O'Grady.

5 p.m.

It is not over! Justin has called. He was not trying to win Sophie back. He was asleep. It is because he is in Sixth Form and it is compulsory to lie in a black-painted bedroom until at least 3 p.m. at weekends and school holidays, preferably listening to gloomy music and reading Jack Kerouac. Although Justin only reads *What Guitar* and graphic novels (aka comics), which is why we are totally across a divide, as I am currently reading *Nineteen Eighty-Four*. It is excellent and all about Room 101 and Big Brother, which is odd as I did not think George Orwell got reality TV. Anyway. I am totally in love. We are meeting tomorrow at his mock-Tudor mansion on Debden Road. I do not want him coming round here yet. Mum will ban him for sure. He has long hair and has done 'It' (allegedly). Oh God. What if he wants me to do 'It'? Know nothing about sex. Except dubious facts gleaned from *a*) PE teacher Miss Beadle (overweight, facial hair, bulgy eyes like Joey in *Friends* or rabbits with myxomatosis) and her plastic penis model and *b*) Thin Kylie and her unnecessary details about Mark Lambert and his very real and active penis. Am going to have to get help from Scarlet's mum and dad Suzy (TV sex counsellor) and Bob (abortionist) fast. Or at least by sixteenth birthday.

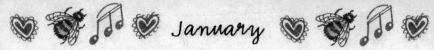

January

New Year Resolutions:

1. Prove that Justin is the ONE by having excellent relationship on every level—brain as well as pant-covered parts.

2. Do not, under any circumstances, let brain or pant-covered parts start thinking about Jack.

3. Do 'It'. And in earth-shattering, meaningful manner. Not on a giant bag of potatoes round the back of the Co-op, like Fat Kylie. Because, as Sad Ed says, sex is not just sweaty thrusting, but is actual, in fact, MEANING OF LIFE.

4. Rekindle Mum and Dad's romance. Do not want to end up in care. It may be utterly tragic and could possibly write best-selling memoir about inevitable mental torture but they might send me somewhere in Harlow, which is at least an hour from Justin by public transport (people in care do not have convenient Passat-driving dads to ferry them to Barratt homes).

5. Get Saturday job so can buy vintage outfits suitable for girlfriend of rock god. And not at Mr Patel's or will end up putting on two stone in Kit Kats like Anita Nolan.

6. Take dog to training classes. Am sick of it devouring possessions and lounging hairily around on sofa when it should be eating Pal and sitting neatly in kennel.

Yes, that is definite recipe for year of utter LOVE. Hurrah.

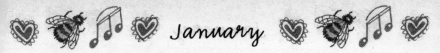

10 p.m.

Have just remembered other essential resolution:

7. Pass GCSEs. Or will end up sweeping up hair with the Kylies at Curl Up and Dye. Or, worse, Mum will disown me and send me to live with inbred Cornish relatives and will have to eat Fray Bentos pies and say 'that it be' a lot.

Tuesday 2

9 a.m.

Hurrah. Am going round Justin's this afternoon for breakfast (his, not mine, have already consumed essential brain and heart stimulating Shreddies). Have just six hours to plan wardrobe and hair, and revise essential snogging tips. Have texted for reinforcements i.e. Scarlet and Sad Ed.

10 a.m.

Scarlet has texted back to say she will be over at one for lunch and summit meeting and can Mum not try to conceal ham in her quiche again. Sad Ed has not texted back. Maybe he is getting in practice at lying in bed for hours for Sixth Form next year. Or more probably he is fiddling with Tuesday under the covers. His mum is totally gullible. She thinks they are having a *Famous Five*-style sleepover when in fact they are doing very non-Enid Blyton things.

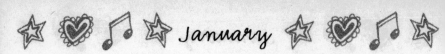
11 a.m.

James's frogs have escaped again. He is very excited as it means they have worked out how to act as one giant frog force to push up the lid of the aquarium. He thinks they may be magic frogs, like the Ninja Turtles. He has renamed them in honour. Mum is not so excited. She says they are going back to Petworld as soon as they are located.

11.15 a.m.

Mum has found Donatello. He was in the toilet (again), making a break for freedom (or trying to get back to sewer headquarters, according to James).

11.30 a.m.

Michaelangelo located in kitchen in half drunk cup of tea. Mum is livid—she says he could have given Marjory next door a heart attack if he had stuck his head out of the PG Tips during their tea and chat session (i.e. moaning about the Britchers' woeful lack of interest in their front garden, and whether or not the BBC should look to a remake of *To The Manor Born* to boost its ratings.)

2 p.m.

Oh God. There has been a terrible accident. Scarlet has trod on a frog, possibly Leonardo. He is clearly not magic. He is just very squashy and dead. She says it was like stamping on slightly crunchy jelly. Am going to definitely wear slippers from now on. A bit of him got stuck between her toes. We

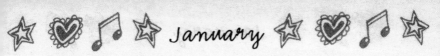

flushed rest down toilet. Will tell James he must have made it back to sewer HQ (not a total lie). He will be devastated if he knows he is a victim of our haste to find hair mousse. Scarlet is lying down on my bed with the curtains drawn. She says it is the most traumatic thing to happen to her since Gordon and Tony (cats, not ageing politicians) ate her gerbils. She says she cannot possibly dispense snogging or wardrobe advice under such circumstances. Have only got one hour to go before I have to meet Justin. Am going to go for a very innocent and covered-up look in the hope he will delay any sexual interest until I have managed to glean advice from Scarlet. Will wear one-armed fluffy jumper (it's a look, sort of) and denim mini, with Oxfam fleece-lined boots. (Which are almost like Uggs, except for the Clarks label inside. So will not be taking them off, obviously.) Hair is successfully less Leo Sayer, due to use of entire can of mousse.

3 p.m.
Raphaelo still missing. Plus Mum has demanded to know provenance of frog-like stain on stair carpet. I said it is an utter mystery but probably something to do with the dog. (I know this is unfair, but the dog is an easy target. He is nearly always the cause of any hoo-ha so one more incident won't affect his record.) James is demanding that we take the dog to the vet's for an autopsy to find the missing frogs. I said I could not get involved in the discussion as I had to go out, and that Scarlet was meditating upstairs and not to disturb

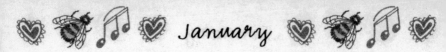

her. James demanded to know where I was going and what time I would be back. I said it was a band rehearsal (not a complete lie, he might do some guitar-playing to woo me) and I would be back by *Eggheads*. (James's favourite TV quiz. He has written in twice offering to take them on single-handedly but the BBC have been strangely quiet in their response.)

3.05 p.m.
Oh God. Cannot believe have used word 'woo'. Sexual education cannot come fast enough. Or maybe it makes me like Elizabeth Bennet. Yes. That is it. I am repressed rural beauty who will be awakened magnificently by cosmopolitan and sexually experienced (two times, allegedly) Mr Darcy, i.e. Justin Statham. Hurrah.

6 p.m.
Was not totally *Pride and Prejudice*-style awakening thing. We watched his Led Zeppelin DVDs for three hours. Admittedly it was in his bedroom (not black, actually pale blue with racing car border), and we did do some excellent snogging when they played 'Whole Lotta Love' (no groping due to vastness of jumper and inability to find entry point). But it is early days. I predict he will be flinging me manfully against his Angus Young posters by the end of the week.

Scarlet was still meditating when I got back. She asked how it was and what he had touched. I said it was

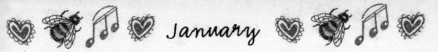

seminal and that he had touched only my heart. She will not understand our love. It is too poetic.

James is still two frogs down. The dog definitely got one after all so I feel no guilt. On the plus side, Mum has agreed to let Michaelangelo and Donatello stay, on the grounds that they no longer have the power to lift the lid up. James is happy. He thinks they will devise a new and Ninja-like way of escaping, so they can fulfil their destiny of fighting Shredder.

Wednesday 3

Am going to fulfil New Year Resolution number 5 and get a Saturday job. Will present myself at shops in Saffron Walden and offer my services. Am going to forsake vintage clothing for a day and wear more business-like outfit, i.e. school uniform, and target Waitrose, as they pay more than minimum wage and also you get a discount in John Lewis, which will please Mum, and free past-their-sell-by cakes, which will please James. Sad Ed is coming with me. He is also looking for work to fund his Mars bar and condom requirements. I do not think he will get a job. He is notoriously lazy and dishevelled. Mum is not entirely backing my job search. She says it could cost me my GCSEs. I said the only cost involved was the increasing one of vintage clothing due to Oxfam getting wise to trendsetting celebrities and raising the price of their Sixties rail to £20, and if she wanted to up my pocket money then she could do so. She said no.

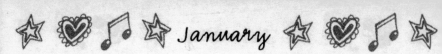

Then James took the opportunity to ask if he could get a job as the frogs were costing a lot in meat (they are strictly non-vegetarian). Mum said he could earn himself 50p by cleaning the dog's teeth. He accepted; it is her highest offer yet. He has been ripped off though. The dog has bad breath.

5 p.m.

Have found job. It is not at Waitrose. They only had one vacancy and it was herding trolleys so they gave it to Sad Ed. I said that was sexist but they said it was more weightist, as he had the hefty upper arm requirement. Yes, and slightly distant expression. My job is at lentil-smelling health food outlet Nuts In May, run by hunchback Mr Goldstein and his ailment-ridden assistant Rosamund. I am going to be stacking carob bars and tofu. On the plus side, they have a pro-vintage clothing policy (Rosamund wears only hessian skirts and hemp blouses) and the shop is opposite Goddard's Butcher's, so I will be able to catch a glimpse of Justin hacking chops through the Linda McCartney display. They are paying me £2.70 an hour. Which is barely legal. But is better than Mum. Justin says we can meet for lunch (and a snog) at one in the Mocha. Hurrah.

Thursday 4

Went round Justin's for more Led Zeppelin watching and snogging. His mum was doing *Rosemary Conley*

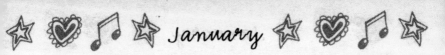

Ultimate Workout in the living room in a mauve leotard and footwarmers. She is frighteningly fit. Justin says she is determined to keep the body of a twenty year old for as long as possible. I asked him how old she was. She is forty-three. Maybe that is what Mum needs to win Dad back. I will suggest it.

3 p.m.
Suggested that Mum joins the gym. She says she is not wasting £45 a month to writhe around on the carpet in someone's else's sweat to 'bangy-bangy' music. Nor will she take up swimming as the pool has a notoriously high urine content. But she is considering calming yoga at the Bernard Evans Youth Centre. It is a step in the right direction, i.e. down the path of love.

Friday 5

10 a.m.
Am not seeing Justin today. I have told him it is essential that I spend quality time with friends (according to *Cosmopolitan*), and make it clear to them that they are of equal priority. Especially in case he chucks me and I will totally need them then (did not say that bit to him, obviously). Am going to invite them for general hanging out in bedroom and moaning about school starting on Monday.

15

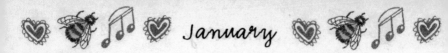

11 a.m.

Scarlet has gone to the London Dungeon with Trevor on a goth pilgrimage and Sad Ed is grounded because Mrs Thomas has discovered the X-rated nature of the *Famous Five* sleepovers. She came in with a midnight feast of scones (at 8 p.m.) and caught them doing some 'exploring', and not on Kirrin Island. Am going round Justin's after all. It is not my fault if friends do not want to be prioritized.

5 p.m.

Did forty-three minutes of snogging and read four *Batman* comics. Tried to initiate conversation on *Pride and Prejudice* but Justin got all excited about Keira Knightley and made me watch *Pirates of the Caribbean* instead. Johnny Depp needs some voice coaching lessons. He was barely understandable. Mrs Statham was doing *Davina Power of Three* today. She has an entire wall devoted to celebrity fitness DVDs including *Dancercise* with someone out of *EastEnders* and *Pole Dancing with the Dingles*. I asked her who was best. She said Kylie's *Hotpants Workout*, if you could get round the gold lamé shorts. Asked if I could borrow it for Mum. She said yes but she needs it back by a week Monday so she can 'pump up her glutes' for her dirty weekend at Champneys with Mr Statham.

7 p.m.

Mum refusing to do *Hotpants* workout. She has booked

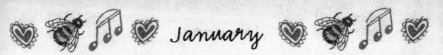

herself in for over-forties yoga at the Bernard Evans Youth Centre tomorrow.

9 p.m.
Oh God. Have just witnessed horrific sight. James is attempting to firm his buttocks with Kylie. Except he has the sound turned down and Classic FM on instead. Mum is doing crap yoga practice at the same time. It is like a scene from a Stanley Kubrick film. Thank God they are fully clothed or I might well need counselling. Also thank God Dad is round at Clive's looking at the new cornicing. He would be ruling dirty weekends out of his diary for good. Ugh. Just did shudder at thought of Mum and Dad doing 'It'. Maybe they don't any more. Maybe they just read Jeffrey Archer books in bed and argue about the dog. I don't know which is worse.

11 p.m.
Can hear Kylie's *Hotpants Workout* music downstairs. Oh God. Think Dad may be watching it for non-fitness reasons. Will investigate.

11.15 p.m.
Was not Dad. Was Grandpa Riley, who had let himself in to 'borrow' (i.e. steal) a pint of milk for Baby Jesus, as the so-called twenty-four-hour garage shuts at ten. Told him to go home before Mum caught him ogling bottoms. He did as he was told. He is frightened of Mum at the best of times.

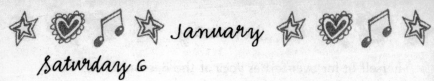

Saturday 6

7 a.m.

First day in world of work. Am very excited. I have to be in at half past eight to restock the lentil bins. Am going to fortify myself with a bacon sandwich. It will be the last meat I get to smell for a whole day. Unless you count the odour of raw pig oozing from Goddard's.

6 p.m.

Am utterly exhausted after day of lugging sacks of muesli around (with help from neither Mr Goldstein (hunchback) nor Rosamund (eczema on fingers)). Plus had to listen to Rosamund talk about her various ailments for eight hours. As well as eczema, she has hot flushes, cold feet, tennis elbow, and ringing in her ears. And hairy legs (she did not mention that one, it is just an observation). She is on twenty-seven vitamin supplements, beating Mum. Did not get to meet Justin at Mocha at one either. The sausage machine was on the blink and he was struggling to hand stuff four kilos of pork meat into a sheep's stomach thingy. Went to watch Sad Ed heave trolleys around in a brown overall instead. He was under the supervision of former Criminal and Retard Gary Fletcher who has been moved from the pet food aisle after getting caught eating Bonio. Sad Ed says he is finding his work less than stimulating. I said all prospective suicidal musicians have to do dead-end jobs, it is a rite of passage. That seemed to cheer him up

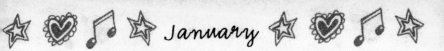
and he went to collect a fleet of trolleys from the top of the multi-storey while Gary smoked a Bensons behind a Volvo and I ate a prawn sandwich. Got paid £18.90. But minus the prawn sandwich, and the giant chocolate cookie, and the copy of *Vogue* (essential for looking vintage and mature), now have just over £10, which will not even buy me a kaftan sleeve in Oxfam. I may well write to the Prime Minister to demand a minimum wage for Saturday girls.

Got home to find Baby Jesus watching *Lovejoy* repeats with Dad and James. Grandpa and Treena are going on belated honeymoon to the Canaries and forgot to book him a ticket (so they claim), and Dad has agreed to look after him for the fortnight. Mum is still out at yoga and knows nothing of this arrangement. I predict she will be less than thrilled.

6 p.m.
Mum is back but is not at all calmed by her yogic experience. She and Dad have had a heated debate and he is now driving Baby Jesus to the airport at top speed in the hope that the flight has been delayed/cancelled. Mum has instructed him to pay whatever the airline demands for a ticket. She has also cancelled all future yoga classes. She says she is not wasting £5 a week to listen to Barbara Marsh chant and make bee noises.

7 p.m.
Flight not delayed. Mum is cursing British Airways. She is angry they have chosen this one day not to have a baggage

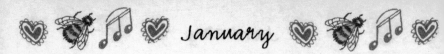
handling crisis or terrorist threats. James pointed out the positive side though—she has two weeks to instil her strict regime on Baby Jesus. He will be off the crisps and cartoons and on to health-giving rice cakes and jolly phonics in days.

Sunday 7

7 a.m.
Jesus is up and demanding television (by clinging to it lovingly and saying 'mmm'). Mum is refusing to switch it on. She has put him on the floor with a selection of Ladybird books and some educational Duplo. I do not think he will be brainwashed this easily. He is used to the perpetual sound of *Jeremy Kyle*.

7.15 a.m.
The television is on. Jesus managed to destroy all the books and feed several pieces of Duplo to the dog. (I do not envy him having to poo it out. The pieces are enormous and pointy.) Mum is making him watch CBeebies though, instead of his preferred ITV and shopping channels.

7.20 a.m.
Jesus has changed the TV to ITV2. He is obviously highly trained in the use of remote controls.

7.25 a.m.
TV back on CBeebies.

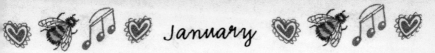
7.30 a.m.
TV on ITV2.

7.35 a.m.
TV back on CBeebies and remote control hidden under sofa.

7.40 a.m.
Remote control missing. Dog shouted at and banished to shed, as usual.

7.45 a.m.
TV back on shouting inbred channel.

7.50 a.m.
Thorough search of Jesus has revealed remote control stashed in Babygro. Dog released from shed and allowed to listen to his favourite CD (Bonnie Tyler's greatest hits) as way of apology. Mum says Jesus may have gone too far down the road of criminality to be rescued. I said Supernanny didn't give up this easily, in the hope this would bait her into further action, but she just sighed wearily and shut herself in the kitchen with *The Archers* and some Fruit 'n' Fibre.

4 p.m.
Went round Sad Ed's to escape clutches of Jesus. He is worse than the dog at stealing or eating valuables. So far, he has managed to post one of Dad's credit cards down a

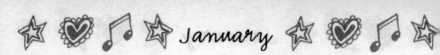
crack in the skirting board, broken a porcelain deer (James's and vile) and eaten four liquorice pipes (Dad's and also vile). Only the dog is happy. It appears positively angelic in comparison and is enjoying a relatively shout-free day. Ed has spent his wages (£21.50, i.e. more than me, but then he does have to wear unflattering brown and talk to Gary Fletcher) on a Joy Division CD, a copy of Sartre's *Nausea*, and packet of condoms (pineapple flavour). I said he should think about saving for the future, but he said there is no point as he is still planning an untimely death. Mrs Thomas made us keep the bedroom door open. I do not know why. There is no way I want to explore Sad Ed's nether regions.

School starts tomorrow. Hurrah. I will be able to see Justin every day and we can snog outside the Sixth Form common room, which will buy me loads of kudos with the lower school—they are easily impressed. Although it will be the first time I have seen Jack since the wardrobe incident. According to Scarlet he is immersing himself in his drums. I expect he will have forgiven me and Justin. He will not let his thwarted love threaten the musical genius of Certain Death.

8 p.m.
Not that Jack loves me.

9 p.m.
And, even if he did, it is not true love as he is utterly not my ONE and am going to stop writing now in case brain or pant-covered parts start wandering.

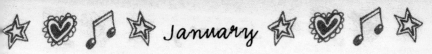

January

Monday 8

Back to school. Mr Wilmott gave us a talk in assembly about how it is a crucial year for all of us and it is time we knuckled down etc., etc. He is right. I am absolutely going to knuckle down. Although it is hard to concentrate in French when Justin is playing football outside in his shorts. He is doing eight resits and AS level PE. He says it is a cinch. All you have to do to pass is know the off-side rule and run around the sheep field in less than fifteen minutes.

Saw Jack outside the mobile science labs. He nodded and said, 'All right, Riley?' I said I was totally fine and asked after Marie-Claire (his annoying Pantene-haired French model girlfriend whom he was snogging prior to the wardrobe incident). He said it was over, and that he is concentrating on his career, as A levels are only eighteen months away and he needs at least five As so he can go to Cambridge and become Foreign Secretary and win the Mercury Music Prize. I said that I too was concentrating on my work. He said, 'Yeah, right, which subject, French KISSING?' He is being very childish. That is the sort of humour I expect from Mark Lambert or any of the O'Gradys. Not from someone who has read Proust and actually understood it.

Also Jack and Justin were not hanging out together at lunch. Jack got Bombay mix out of the nut-dispensing machine and Justin went to Mr Patel's for Wotsits.

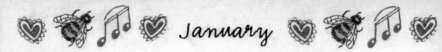
5 p.m.

Jesus has broken the washing machine. He climbed inside so that he could poke Rice Krispies through all the little holes.

Tuesday 9

James has a black eye. Mum is furious and says he cannot play with Mad Harry any more. But James said it is not Mad Harry or Stephen 'Maggot' Mason, who eats mud. There is a new gang leader at St Regina's Primary. It is Keanu, the youngest and deadliest O'Grady boy. He has taken over the playground and is now ranked first toughest in the infants.

Wednesday 10

James is refusing to go to school in case Keanu duffs him up again. Asked him how old Keanu was. He is five. But he has a weight advantage and menacing earrings. Mum says he is going to school, Keanu or no Keanu, as she is struggling to cope with the dog and Jesus as it is, and doesn't want James lurking about as well. This is not like her. She is usually itching to have a go at an O'Grady. Jesus is obviously taking up the entire anti-anti-social behaviour bit of her brain.

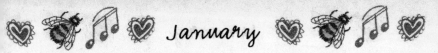

4 p.m.

There has been a crisis in the world of rock. Certain Death have split up! Jack told Justin this morning. He claims it is because of artistic differences but I fear it is all over me. I am like Layla in that song and they are Eric Clapton and that one out of the Beatles that died and isn't John Lennon. Justin says he is not worried. He predicts Jack will be begging him to come back by the end of the week as no one else in Saffron Walden can play more than four chords or has access to a Transit van.

Also James has another Keanu-inflicted injury. It is a Peperami inserted up his nose. Mum has relented and is going in tomorrow to talk to Reverend Begley. It is not so much the violence, more because James said the Peperami smelt nice and she doesn't want him falling into the clutches of junk food.

Thursday 11

Asked Scarlet about Certain Death during Rural Studies (drawing pictures of chickens). Scarlet says Jack is branching out in a new direction, music-wise. Asked her if he was branching out love-wise. She said he is definitely off women now that Marie-Claire has chucked him because he told her she was not the ONE. I asked Scarlet if she knew who the ONE was. She says it is his drum kit—all top musicians are married to their music

25

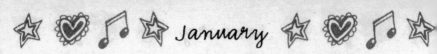

first and their women second, that is why they are such inconsiderate lovers. She got that from Suzy who once did it with one of Duran Duran's roadies. Lesson abandoned early due to Mark Lambert letting live chicken models out onto C Corridor and whole class having to round them up before they infiltrated the ventilation shafts like last year.

Mum is livid. Reverend Begley is refusing to do anything about the Keanu situation. He says he is going to let it run its course, i.e. wait for someone else to duff Keanu up and take over again. It is because he is scared of Mrs O'Grady. Mum says it is like *Lord of the Flies* in the playground at St Regina's.

Friday 12

Hurrah. Got detention for snogging Justin in the upper school boys' toilets when should have been in library pretending to read Maths text book (as if). Am totally rebellious and my reputation as lover of ace guitarist will be all round school by Monday and will get canteen privileges and the respect of all Year Seven EMOs.

4 p.m.

Saw Jack on way home after detention. He was talking to Justin's ex Sophie Jacobs (of big nipple perversion) outside Mr Patel's. They were obviously telling jokes because they

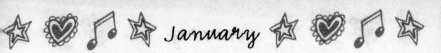
laughed hysterically as I walked past. I did not say hello. I am above their puerile humour.

James is suspiciously injury free. Asked him about it when Mum was changing Jesus's nappy (it is best to stay outside a three-room radius due to shrieking and flying faeces). Apparently he and Mad Harry have bowed to demands and are now acting as minders to Keanu. He says it is the only way to survive the cut-throat world of a Church of England primary school.

Saturday 13

Work. Mum and James came in to buy mung bean seeds for her cultivator and Nuts In May patented oat and raisin bars for Jesus, to wean him off Kit Kats. She has no chance; I have tasted one and they are like chewy gravel. Rosamund has developed a new ailment—it is head lice. Offered to run to Boots to get her some louse-eliminating chemicals but she says she prefers the natural method of tea tree oil and a nit comb. Spent rest of day avoiding her (bottom-length) plaits.

Met Justin for lunch on the bench in the market square (broken pork pies, courtesy of Mr Goddard—at least it saves my minuscule wages). He is getting restless, music-wise. He says he is giving Jack until Monday to beg him to come back to Certain Death and then he will have to consider Plan B. Asked him what Plan B was. He said he hadn't planned it yet.

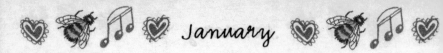

6 p.m.

Mum has asked if I am 'courting'. Marjory spotted me on the bench while she was buying a sink plunger in Gayhomes (not homosexualist shop, but crap hardware one). Plus the toilet snogging rumour had reached her via school secretary Mrs Leech (bad hair; too much face powder; biscuit habit) who told her cousin Enid who told Mrs Carter from number 47 who told Mum in the queue at Barclays. Denied everything. It is essential teenage behaviour to conceal love life from parents. Plus Mum will try to talk to me about 'urges' if she finds out I am snogging a rock god, which will be potentially hideous.

Sunday 14

Justin has rung. He is in shock. Jack has got a new band. They are called the Jack Stone Five, which is ironic, apparently, as there are only four of them, and they have got a gig next month at the Air Training Corps hut (youth group for the criminally weapons-obsessed). Asked Justin how they are managing without his transport options but apparently they have got Matthew Quinn on bass, whose dad has a fish delivery van. Justin says he is going to form a better band. Am going round his to think up names after lunch.

7 p.m.

Band still unnamed. My suggestions of Ambient Monkey and Cats Don't Wear Pants utterly rejected. Also it has

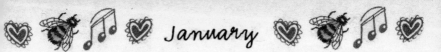
no members except Justin. I have offered to do vocals but Justin said he was going to put an advert in *NME*. I suggested the A Corridor noticeboard might be better. We are going to reconvene after school on Wednesday in the mobile music room with potential members. Sad Ed says he is definitely auditioning. Although, if he gets in, which will be a miracle, frankly, given his fat fingers, it may only split the Jack v. Justin camp further with Scarlet on one side of the artistic divide and me, Sad Ed, and Tuesday on the other.

Monday 15

Oh my God. Tuesday is IN the Jack Stone Five. She is lead vocals and tambourine. She is totally overexcited and is planning her stage outfits already. She is going for a Blondie meets Bat for Lashes look (i.e. slutty fortune teller). Sad Ed says they will not let it affect their love life. They are going to be utterly grown-up and keep business separate from pleasure. Plus he says it may heal the divide between John Major High and the Quaker school that Tuesday is forced to go to and we will be able to mingle freely instead of hurling *Chewits* at each other across the High Street.

8 p.m.
Sad Ed rang. Tuesday is not speaking to him because he said she sounds more like a choirgirl than Courtney Love.

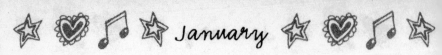

January

He has suggested Justin gets Tuesday's Quaker friend Daisy Truelove Jones on vocals to annoy her. Plus Daisy's dad runs BJ Video (aka Blow Job Video) and can get us free DVDs.

Tuesday 16

The Certain Death split is causing havoc at the Alternative Music Club lunch table. Die-hard Certain Death fans (several Year Eights and Stan Barrett who once saw Paul Weller in John Lewis) are refusing to let any of the Jack Stone Five or their minions sit with them. So they have commandeered the table by the fire extinguishers (formerly Goth Corner). And now the goths are up in arms as they are bored with Goth Corner Mark II (next to woefully empty trophy cabinet) and want to move back to their old table. Luckily Mrs Brain got annoyed with all the rearranging and threatened everyone with her doughnut tongs (disused due to Jamie Oliver enforcement of fruit eating).

Also Jesus has released the frogs. Mum says she only took her eye off him for a second. James gave her a withering look and said, 'That second could be the difference between life and death. You should know better.' Mum said she was distracted by the dog trying to dig a hole in the stair carpet. Jesus is now in quarantine (in his cot) while the house is forensically swept for Michaelangelo and Donatello.

30

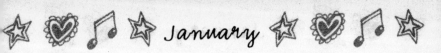

6.30 p.m.

Frogs located in cot. Jesus had been hoarding them in his nappy. Mum says the wetness may have been their lifeline. James has washed them with Carex though. He is not taking any cross-infection chances.

Wednesday 17

8 a.m.

Hurrah. It is our inaugural band meeting tonight. Note use of 'our'. I am sure to get starring role, as am Justin's girlfriend. Maybe will not have to do GCSEs after all but will be attend university of life and learn how to affect a cockney accent and learn how to drink five pints of cider without vomiting. Sad Ed and several Alternative Music Table members are coming. Scarlet is refusing unless he can give her assurances that they will include Marilyn Manson as one of their influences. Justin says he cannot give her that peace of mind. Our first point of business is the name. I have an excellent new suggestion—The Banned. It is utterly clever. Plus all excellent bands have a 'the' in the title. Like The Editors. And The Strokes.

8.15 a.m.

But not The Wurzels. Obviously.

8.17 a.m.

Or Editors apparently.

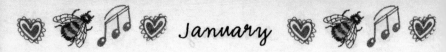

6 p.m.

The band is not called The Banned. It is 'Don't Let the Pigeon Drive the Bus'. It is Stan Barrett's idea and is named after his favourite book. Also am not lead vocals. Or even in band, exactly. Justin says he does not want anyone thinking we are ripping off the Jack Stone Five with a girl as the front man. He is going to do vocals and lead guitar. Stan Barrett is on bass, Dean 'the dwarf' Denley is on drums, and Sad Ed is on second guitar, on the proviso that he only plays when he actually knows the chords. I am going to do promotion and management. Which Justin says is better than being in band. He is right. I will be like leprechaunish impresario Louis Walsh, and will make millions from my ability to spot raw talent.

Why is head itching?

7 p.m.

Oh God. Have got head lice. Mum caught me scratching during *Look East* and did a forensic check. It is Rosamund's fault. They must have leapt across the Well Woman shelf while we were rearranging overpriced organic sanitary towels. Mum has banished me to the bathroom with several bottles of chemicals (she has no concern for the environment, her only goal is to be pest-free). But cannot get nit comb through gigantic hairdo so now have millions of dead lice clinging to hair. It is like the killing fields of Baghdad. Or wherever they were. Am considering shaven look. Although Justin will chuck me for sure. Oh God. What

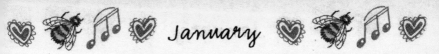

if I have given them to Justin during one of our snogging sessions. They may have wandered carelessly across onto his rock star hairdo. The shame.

8 p.m.
Dead nits are out. Mum did it. Am in agony. She is ruthless with her comb technique. Will check Justin surreptitiously tomorrow.

Thursday 18

Tried to check Justin's hair during band meeting at lunch (crucial decision—do we want the O in 'Don't' to be shaped like a skull or is that just naff. Conclusion—naff, it is going to be the pigeon's eye instead) but he was wearing a hat (de rigueur in Sixth Form for aspiring Kurt Cobain types). Am going to resort to Plan B (unlike Justin, I actually have one) and blame any potential scratching on Oona Rickets. She is notoriously unclean. Anyway, have far more pressing things than nits to worry about. Justin's mum and dad are going on their dirty weekend to Champneys on Saturday (his and hers massages, colonic irrigation, and romantic carrot stick dinners) and he has asked me to stay over, which is boy speak for 'do It'. Have to think of excuse not to go. Am still hopelessly unschooled in what goes where and when, plus am not legal and may get exposed by *Daily Mail* or something. Will think up Plan A, and Plan B as matter of emergency.

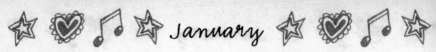
Friday 19

8 a.m.
I think the lice menace may have spread. I caught James scratching over his toast and Marmite. Did not mention it to Mum as do not want to be punished as source of outbreak.

4 p.m.
James has been sent home from school with lice. He is not ashamed. Apparently Keanu has had them twenty-five times and also has semi-permanent ringworm.

4.15 p.m.
Dad has been sent home early with lice. In stark contrast to James's devil-may-care attitude, he is entirely ashamed. Mr Wainwright, his boss, saw one walking around his collar in a meeting about the coffee machine. Mum has ordered everyone to form an orderly queue at the bathroom door. She is doing Jesus and the dog as well, as precautionary measures.

Saturday 20

Work. Another seven hours with Rosamund and her parasites beckons. Also am supposed to be going round Justin's tonight for sex and still have no Plan A or Plan B to get out of it other than feigning death or claiming to

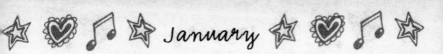

January

be religious. Will text Scarlet, she has a year's worth of experience of fending off Trevor's sexual advances. They were planning on doing 'It' at the winter solstice but at the last minute she told him her biorhythms were all wrong and they would have to defer until Hallowe'en.

1 p.m.
Mr Goldstein has turned my mobile phone off. It is at Rosamund's request in case the radiation gives her cancer. Am going to see Sad Ed on trolleys instead in the hope he has some words of wisdom. Will tell Justin I am out on Nuts In May business and he will have to eat his reject pork pies on his own today.

1.30 p.m.
Sad Ed too busy inventing time travel with Gary Fletcher. He is going to get the sack soon if he is not careful. So now have six and a half hours to think of way to retain virginity. Obviously could just say no, as recommended by PE teacher and 'sexpert' Miss Beadle, but do not want to get reputation as prude or lezzer.

6 p.m.
Hurrah! Am not going to have to have sex after all. It is because Mum has incontrovertible evidence of me and Justin snogging behind the Passat (digital photos by Marjory. She should set up her own detective agency—neither of us heard any rustling in the privet) and has banned me from

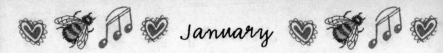

January

going over there except under strict adult supervision. I have never been so happy at her medieval regime. Phoned Justin to tell him. He is less thrilled. Not even when I told him we were totally like Romeo and Juliet. I said we could meet in secret at dawn on Barry Island (car park on Common where O'Gradys go to rev up their Datsuns) but he said he would be asleep and would see me at school on Monday. He is just annoyed at having to suppress his urges. I think it is all utterly tragic and romantic. Will watch *Casualty* with excellent air of thwarted teenage sexuality, i.e. sulking and huffing a lot. Will also drop 'you've forgotten what it's like' into conversation somewhere. Although suspect Mum never knew what it is like. The only time she is overcome with passion is when she has a bottle of Cillit Bang in her hand.

Sunday 21

11 a.m.

Grandpa and Treena get back this afternoon. You can tell Mum is happy because she has let James set up a frog assault course in the bath. He is training them for their potential death match with Shredder. They have to scale down the flannels, drop onto his plastic submarine, sail to the plughole and finish by jumping over an arrangement of Head and Shoulders bottles. There is no way they are going to complete it.

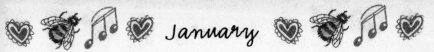

11.30 a.m.

I take it back. The frogs have completed their challenge and are being rewarded by bits of off-cut organic lamb (i.e. Sunday lunch). Mum does not know about that part. She is restricting them to second-rate mince but James says a high quality diet is crucial to their world domination powers.

2 p.m.

Jesus has been repatriated to Harvey Road. Grandpa and Treena picked him up after lunch. Although it turns out they have been home for three days but could not be bothered to get him. Mum does not care. Those three days were crucial in her battle to save Jesus from sin.

6 p.m.

Grandpa has rung to say Jesus has refused to eat his chocolate Ready Brek and is uncharacteristically watching *Songs of Praise*. Apparently Treena is in complete panic. She can only do toast or heat up things in the microwave, and Aled Jones brings her out in a rash. Mum, on the other hand, is jubilant. Her track record of raising compliant children is back to 100 per cent.

Monday 22

Met Justin for lunch (aka snogging on the sheep field, now that toilets are out of bounds due to possibility of surprise

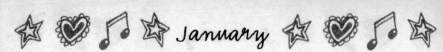

raids by Miss Beadle). He is still sulking about his wasted empty-house opportunity. Asked him whether he had spent the night in torture on his bed. He said, *au contraire*, he had gone round to Tim Newbold's instead to watch *Spiderman*. Am now in panic. Tim is the brother of Pippa Newbold, who is best friend of Sophie Microwave Muffins Jacobs, who is ex-girlfriend of Justin. What if she was there? What if she is over her fat nipple perversion and wants him back? Oh God, he is bound to want her, she is a 34C now (official measurement), which is several sizes bigger than me. Am going to have to improve size of bust if I want to keep Justin. I know he should love me for my intellectual superiority etc., but I fear hefty breasts may trump my freakish ability to recite Kipling.

Also, there has been a nit outbreak at John Major High. The entire upper school was scratching in nondenominational assembly this morning. Asked Mrs Leech casually if she had identified the source yet. She says it is bound to be an O'Grady, or possibly Nigel Moore who once had potato blight. I agreed. Although it was not potato blight. It was impetigo.

Tuesday 23

My life is one perpetual cycle of potentially life-altering decisions. This week it is A-level choices. Have not even started revising for GCSEs yet and we are having to start

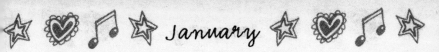

worrying about the next barrage of exams. It is utterly unfair. May well write to the Education Secretary to complain about this culture of constant testing. James has already had three sets of SATs and he is not even ten. Although he says he actually enjoys them and that the only people who dread exams are the weak and the stupid. He got that theory from Mum. We are allowed to take three each plus an AS. Except for Emily Reeve (peanut allergy, knee-length socks (and not an ironic Japanese way), vast doll collection) and the Maths Club geeks who are taking five each and several AS levels. It is because Mr Wilmott thinks it will compensate for the rest of the school who will get Ds and Es if they even bother to show up.

Am going to do English and Drama (so can be either Gwyneth Paltrow or Sylvia Plath, or both, possibly, in a remake of *Sylvia*!), French (we get to go on an exchange, potentially in Paris, world centre of tragic and literary things in general), and AS Philosophy (so can avoid repeat of Year Nine Karl Marx/Marx Brothers mix-up). Sad Ed wanted to do English, Drama, Music, and Art. I said he may be restricting himself career-wise, given his as yet unproven talents in the creative areas (his portrait of Scarlet looked like the one with the pointy ears out of *Lord of the Rings*). He said he is not unproven, just unappreciated. But has swapped English for AS Philosophy none the less. Scarlet is doing English, Politics, Economics, and Philosophy. Justin is not picking any, he is pinning all his post-resit hopes on Rock Foundation at Braintree FE College.

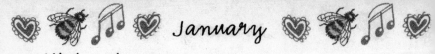

Wednesday 24

Had band rehearsal after school, i.e. watching Sad Ed strum vaguely along to the White Stripes while Justin shouted chord changes at him. At least Dean 'the dwarf' Denley can play the drums, although he has to sit on three cushions and even then you cannot see him over the cymbals.

Justin asked Sad Ed for inside info on the Jack Stone Five's set. He says Tuesday is still not speaking to him about business matters following his questioning of her on-stage presence. Although she is still letting him fiddle with her business areas. They are doing it at Mr Wilmott's house now, as he is notoriously ineffectual when it comes to disciplining teenagers.

Thursday 25

Oh my God. Someone at John Major High is with child, according to Mark Lambert (he did not say 'with child', he said 'up the duff'). He overheard security-unconscious Mrs Leech on the phone to the council while he was waiting to be punished for jamming Dean 'the dwarf' Denley in a toilet (again).

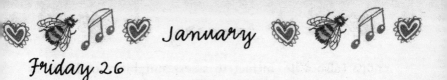

Friday 26

Ali Hassan and the Maths Club geeks have opened a book on the question of the mother-to-be. They were inundated with bets during lunchtime. All fingers point to Fat Kylie and Mr Whippy. She is well known for eschewing contraception, due to her Catholic beliefs, and he is well-known for his inability to keep his 'magic cone' to himself.

Saturday 27

Oh God. The Dad as potential sex-beast situation has reared its ugly head again. Worse, it happened in lentil-smelling Nuts In May in full view of hunchbacked Mr Goldstein and ailment-riddled Rosamund. Dad and Mum had come in to allegedly buy James some Sesame Snaps (in reality, check up on my career as health food outlet assistant) when Edie suddenly appeared from behind the protein supplements looking like an ageing rock star with all manner of excessive eyeliner, tattoos, and come hithering. (Tuesday actually had to tell Edie to cover herself up, something I am unlikely ever to be forced to do with Mum, she thinks knee length skirts are skimpy.) Dad pretended to be far more interested in the eco-friendly deodorant but Mum dragged him out of the shop immediately and into Goddard's on the pretext of buying

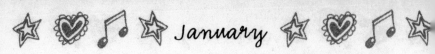

chops (also a lie; in fact to assess suitability of Justin as suitor) without paying for James's health-giving snack. The 36p was docked from my pitiful pay packet. It is lucky Mr Goldstein is so tolerant. (It is his Jewish background. And the hump.) Also he is desperate as there were no other applicants for my job apart from Fat Kylie, who is unemployable. It is also lucky Justin was out the back of Goddard's swilling meat mess down the drain. He is yet to experience Mum's Paxman-like cross-examination technique, and will need special training in how to deflect trick questions.

Why is Edie so interested in Dad? Maybe it is because he is her first love and she has never got over him. Maybe he is her ONE. Oh God. Am so going to be child of broken home, which will utterly ruin my GCSE prospects. On the plus side, Tuesday will be my stepsister and I will get instant access to her wardrobe. It is a fine line.

Texted Justin to see if he wanted to meet in secret after work but he texted back to say he was working on some new material with the band. Offered to come and watch but he said no. He is definitely going off me. Went home immediately to do bust increasing exercises, as demonstrated by Thin Kylie during French oral, and she is a C cup. Measured bust. Still 32A. Maybe it is like Mr Muscle sink unblocker and works overnight. Will just do a few more and go to bed.

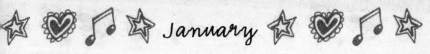
Sunday 28

8 a.m.
Bust still minuscule size. Maybe just need to do more.

10 a.m.
Chest in agony after two hours of continual muscular squeezing. And still only 32A. Plus Mum burst into bedroom to demand what suspicious groaning was. (She has been given the fear by Mrs Thomas.) But her search of potential Justin-concealing places (in bed, under bed, in wardrobe, in shoeboxes (he is not contortionist, as have pointed out, but she is clearly not taking any chances)) proved fruitless so she has gone back to supervising James and Mad Harry who are making toffee apples. I only hope they are intended for consumption and not for use as weaponry by Keanu's playground gang.

Monday 29

Fat Kylie is not pregnant. She got off hockey with period pain this morning. Miss Beadle said menstruation is a normal bodily function, not an excuse to read *Heat* magazine in the changing rooms, but Fat Kylie said, 'Three Tampax an hour ain't normal, miss, and what if it, like, gushes?' Miss Beadle was clearly panicked by Fat Kylie's potential gushing and said she could be referee instead (result 0–0, and teams reduced to two a side with everyone else thrown

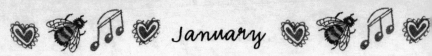

off for 'shitness'). Suspicions now rest with Primark Donna, trainee chavette and little sister of Leanne Jones, notorious free giver of sexual favours. The Maths Club are going to interview her at the first opportunity.

Tuesday 30

James has been given a gang nickname by Keanu—it is 'Brains'. Asked what Mad Harry's was. He said, 'It is Mad Harry, duh.' (He is getting decidedly brattish since his new-found acquaintance with an O'Grady, even if it is in the name of self-preservation.) Why have I never had a nickname? Actually I know why; it is because Mum has forbidden me ever to acquire one. Even shortening of names is strictly out of bounds. Am going to invent one. Will drop it into conversation until people have forgotten I was ever called Rachel.

8 p.m.
Have shortlisted nicknames, with aid of 'Brains' Riley:
- Books (as am literary goddess)
- Hack (potential journalistic career, though possibly also makes me sound like machete murderer)
- Ray (cool and slightly androgenous, à la Andie in *Pretty in Pink*)
- R'n'R (James's favourite due to similarity to pasty-faced rap genius Eminem though makes me sound backward

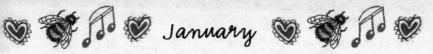

with all the 'arring')
Think will go for Ray. Will start usage tomorrow.

Wednesday 31

It is my and Justin's one-month anniversary, which is positively long-term by John Major High standards. We are meeting after school for a celebratory snog. Also have got him a card. And signed it from Ray! Scarlet asked if he had told me he loved me yet. I said not exactly, but almost. She said how exactly. I said he said he loved the way my hair sproinged back no matter how hard you squished it down. She said that is not the same thing at all. Sad Ed says he is probably waiting until he has 'tested all the goods'. I said that our love was above matters of the flesh. It is more spiritual. Except that I am not sure that is entirely the case. He has shown no interest in my suggestion of reading Rossetti poems to each other on the banks of (admittedly shopping-trolley-clogged) Slade river. But maybe playing Xbox is a modern meeting of minds. Yes, that is it. Totally.

5 p.m.
Had excellent snog with Justin down Battleditch Lane (aka Dogshit Alley). Gave him my card. He said, 'You've spelt your name wrong, Riley.' I am not disheartened. Nicknames take weeks to embed. Like investigative journalists.

I'm RACHEL RILEY
— welcome to my so-called life.

February

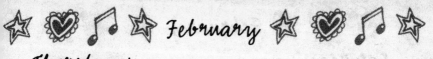

Thursday 1

It is Glastonbury registration day. Me, Sad Ed, Tuesday and Justin are all going to put ourselves on the list. Scarlet and Jack do not have to stoop to such measures. It is because Suzy knows the Eavis man with the Amish hairdo and gets free tickets and a pass to the VIP toilet area every year. Sad Ed has taken photos of us all with his mobile phone for uploading. His camera is rubbish though. Despite fourteen attempts I still look like a man. Justin does not mind. He says I have the look of someone called Robert Plant about me. Have signed up under my new name Ray Riley. Having a street nickname will totally increase my chance of getting in. Although it is all hypothetical as there is no way Mum will let me go. She thinks I will end up 'smoking ecstasy and juggling'. They are equally evil in her eyes.

Friday 2

My excellent nickname is still not catching on. I texted Scarlet saying 'Meet me in toilets, X Ray' and she went to Mr Wilmott to tell him my phone had been hijacked by sex pest Raymond Jackson (aka X-Ray) in Year Eleven who once asked Scarlet to lick his toes. She did not. They are hobbit-like and possibly fungal.

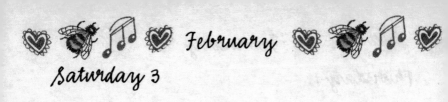
Saturday 3

8 a.m.

Why, oh why, did I get a Saturday job? It is utter torture having to get up at half seven to sell vitamins and mung beans to badly dressed people (i.e. hippies, lesbians, and hypochondriacs) when I could be at home in bed reading life-changing literature, or at least on the sofa watching CBeebies with the dog. Have begged Dad to call in sick for me but he said he did not get where he is today (Financial Adviser to Wainwright and Hogg Office Supplies) by wheedling his way out of his Saturday job. Asked what his Saturday job was—he said he cleaned Grandpa Riley's car for 50p. Anyway, that is not the reason, it is in case Mum finds out. He is driving me there to make sure I do not detour to Scarlet's on the way.

6 p.m.

Work utterly unfulfilling. Monotony punctuated only by getting to snog Justin round the back of the meat bins. Although the smell and bloodstains are a bit offputting. Am consoling myself with thought that all artistic types have to suffer menial jobs and poverty-line pay packets, whilst writing their masterpieces by candlelight. When I am famous they will put a blue plaque on the peeling plaster at Nuts In May saying 'Rachel Riley once toiled here'.

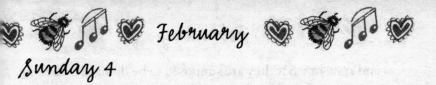

Sunday 4

Granny Clegg rang to check none of us died in the night. It is because her gyppy hip is playing up and she says it is a portent of doom. The last time she got the gripes, three of Hester's chickens keeled over in the night. Mum said we are all very much alive, although the dog is living on borrowed time, as usual. Mum said Granny should get her hip looked at if it is that gyppy, she might get a nice new metal one on the NHS. Granny Clegg said she'd rather have a Disprin. It is because she doesn't like going to the doctors since Dr Trelawney (male, English, ancient, doles drugs out like Smarties) retired and got replaced by Dr Kimber (female, Australian, youthful, prescribes drugs only in proven cases of infection, and only after 'putting up with it for a week' has failed to see an improvement).

Went round Justin's for band practice this afternoon. Gave Sad Ed managerial advice, i.e. to hang guitar lower on strap as it is very high up and makes him look like evangelical music teacher Mr Beston instead of cool one out of Kaiser Chiefs. Also to practise playing as he is still struggling with G and even Mark Lambert can play that. (As evidenced by performance at Mrs Duddy's Annual Retards and Criminals 'We've Got Talent' show. No longer annual due to lack of any discernible talent and abundance of fighting.) Sad Ed said he cannot help it if his arms are disproportionately short and his fingers slightly oversized. Then he demanded that managers (i.e. me) should be banned from rehearsals

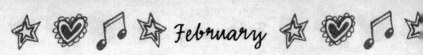
and stick to what they are supposed to be doing, i.e. booking gigs and getting record deals. I said it was imperative to 'understand their sound' if I was going to secure top listing at Bernard Evans Youth Centre. Luckily Justin agreed. Plus he said it is useful to have someone to fetch orange squash and crisps, and to wipe sweat off his brow during guitar solos (he did not say that bit, I just like doing it).

Monday 5

Ali Hassan asked to see my stomach in Citizenship. I threatened to report him to Ms Hopwood-White for perving but he says he is just conducting checks for signs of weight gain. It is for the Maths Club school pregnancy gambling ring. Showed him stomach. He made notes. Demanded to see notes. Demanded to know why I was listed in the possibles category. He said there is definite swelling. I said it is not pregnancy, obviously, it is illicit can of Diet Coke, purchased as love gift by Justin from Mr Patel, and that if swelling is the only criteria then Sad Ed must be a contender. He said there are three categories. The others are first break vomiting and buying tuna surprise off Mrs Brain (only pregnant person could crave this) and they are being cross-referenced at the Maths and Science Club joint AGM on Friday (aka freaks and geeks convention). Noted that Scarlet was on the first break vomiting list. It is not pregnancy, it is because Suzy is away filming her TV sex show and Edna is in charge of breakfast.

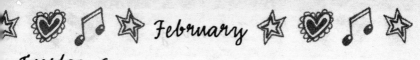

February

Tuesday 6

James got sent home from school early. It is because he and Mad Harry have been refereeing Keanu's new lunchtime Fight Club. He was in his bedroom with the dog when I got home, eating a penitent's tea of crackers and an apple (the dog is being punished for chewing the stairs). I asked him what went on at Fight Club. He said, 'The first rule of Fight Club is that you do not talk about Fight Club.' Mum is right. He is being brainwashed by an O'Grady. I have suggested we call in reinforcements, i.e. his ex-best friend Mumtaz. She would be an excellent calming influence with her Eastern religion and jingly music. Mum is not so sure. She is going to consult Dad on boarding schools. She says St Regina's is in danger of going the way of St Maxentius (closed due to overhigh O'Grady count) and it might be better to get out before it is too late.

Wednesday 7

Dad is refusing to send James to boarding school. He says it is a hotbed of future fascists and perverts. Plus we cannot afford it due to the continual dog-related damage and Mum's appalling clutch control (Fiesta bills already through roof). James is disappointed. He was hoping to be packed off to Eton each term with a tuck box full of home-made jam and Liquorice Allsorts. No chance. Mum would

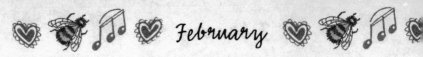

fill it with fluoride tablets and anti-bacterial wipes. It is a relief. Not only would it be reputation ruining in the uber-left-wing Sixth Form to have a relation at boarding school, it would mean Mum's focus was entirely on me, and I rely heavily on James and his frog chaos to divert attention from my minor spillages and misdemeanours.

Thursday 8

Grandpa Riley rang. Jesus said his first word today. It is 'skip'. Mum got excited as it was one of the key words on the flash cards she was terrorizing him with during the honeymoon, but it turns out it was a demand for one of Treena's prawn cocktail crisps. Grandpa is jubilant none the less. He says Baby Jesus is a genius and he is going to get him tested for Mensa. James says they will not let him in. He is just annoyed because he was refused entry last year on grounds of not being boffiny enough. Which is frightening as James can recite all the books of the Bible, and the periodic table, off by heart, in song.

Friday 9

Last day of school. The John Major High pregnancy scandal has been solved, and not by cardigan-wearing (and not in a this-season way) 'mathletes' either, but by Dean 'the dwarf'

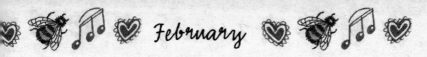

Denley. Mrs Leech and Mr Wilmott were discussing it over custard creams at first break, and had not noticed 'The Dwarf' (as he is now known) standing at the desk waiting to hand in a note (to get off PE on the grounds that he is persistently picked last and has been used as a ball on several occasions). Astonishingly, it is not Primark Donna. It is Emily Reeve! Wearer of knee-length socks and owner of vast doll collection! She is three months gone, i.e. due in crucial GCSE season. This is what happens when your parents do not let you go to sex education with Miss Beadle and her plastic penis, or you do not have access to Thin Kylie and her stack of *Cosmopolitans*.

Scarlet says she has thrown her entire future away for five minutes of fumbling. She is right. Emily will be knee-deep in nappies and vomit while the rest of us are enjoying the high life of Sixth Form. (Also possibly vomit, as Sad Ed pointed out, but not nappies. I hope.) Mr Wilmott is especially outraged. It is because her potential absence will bring down his grade point average and we will be beaten yet again in the league tables by Burger King Sports Academy (formerly the Harold Wilson Modern). The Maths Club are happy though. They have made excellent profits (£37.50, including several stakes from members of staff) and have opened another book on who the father is. It is a good question. I might befriend her and she will confide in me and I can win big. Or refuse to tell and put others off the scent to protect our friendship. She is excellently tragic and Julie Burchillesque after all. Oooh, I could write a novel about it.

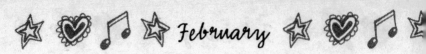

8 p.m.

Just had worrying thought. If Emily Reeve, who wears cagoules and days of the week pants, is doing 'It', then the pressure is piling on me, especially as I wear vintage and own black pants (present from Scarlet and hidden from Mum in Postman Pat moneybox). Although, to be fair, Justin has made no sexual demands on me yet. Maybe he is a New Man and is respecting my body etc. Hurrah.

9 p.m.

Or maybe he does not want to do 'It' with me because I am utterly non-sexual. Oh God. Am absolutely going to devote entire half term to bust expansion.

Saturday 10

Grandpa Riley and Treena visited me at work today with Baby Jesus. Mr Goldstein offered Jesus a 'treat' of dried figs but Jesus just said 'Skip, Skip' repeatedly until Treena fished a bag of them out of the pushchair. Mr Goldstein looked visibly disappointed. I do not blame Jesus though. The figs are vile and look like shrivelled poo. Treena bought Ginseng and Royal Jelly, i.e. sex stimulating products. I am amazed they need any. They are always at it. Unless it is because they are trying for another baby. I hope not. As Mum pointed out, by the time Jesus is ten, Grandpa Riley will probably be dribbling or dead.

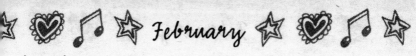
Sunday 11

4 p.m.
Band practice called off on account of the drum section (i.e. The Dwarf) being inconveniently at his Aunty Sheila's for lunch and second guitar (i.e. Sad Ed) being inconveniently at Tuesday's for snogging. Am considering sacking them. I bet Led Zeppelin never had to put up with these sorts of poor excuses. On the plus side, me and Justin got to 'hang' i.e. he played his guitar while I nodded appreciatively at intervals.

I wonder what I would be doing if me and Jack were together instead. Maybe sitting in an arty café sipping red wine and discussing Hegelian Dialectic (as advertised in Head of Philosophy (and hairy librarian) Mr Knox's pro-AS-level flyer). Or buying vintage overcoats together. Oh God. Stop thinking about Jack. He is utterly out of bounds. Plus there are no arty cafés in Saffron Walden; the Mocha just has fruit machines and a velvet Elvis.

4.15 p.m.
And am with love of life i.e. Justin. So do not care about discussing philosophy with random boy.

4.30 p.m.
Oooh. Velvet Elvis would be a good name for a band. It is much catchier than the Pigeon thing.

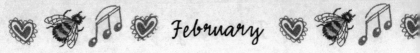

Monday 12
Half term

10 a.m.
Bust increasing endeavours start today (still 32A at last official measure-in at Scarlet's, compared to her 32Bs). Have done twenty minutes of crunching and stretching and am now moving on to googling herbal remedies on James's computer. (Christmas laptop still being 'fixed' by Malcolm 'the geek' at Dad's office.)

11 a.m.
Am pinning hopes on obtaining product called 'Wonderup' instead. It is from Japan and has seven kinds of herbs in it. Ooh, I wonder if Mr Goldstein has it. Maybe he will give it to me at a discount. After all, what is point of working in health product shop if you do not make best use of health boosting (or breast boosting) products.

2 p.m.
Mr Goldstein does not stock Wonderup or Grobust or any other natural breast-enlarging supplements. (It is a wonder he is in business at all really, he does not seem willing to move with the times.) And have no credit card to buy things with over interwebnet so am back to daily exercises.

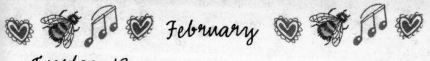
Tuesday 13

James and Mad Harry have offered to 'mesmerize' my bust into growing. (They checked the search history on Internet Explorer and discovered my plight.) Asked what this involved. Mad Harry said he would need to assess the 'size of the problem' first. Declined. Do not want to flash breasts at low-rent Paul McKennas. Especially as one is my brother.

Anyway, am not depressed. Because it is Valentine's Day tomorrow and I do not have to worry about whether or not I will get a card this year as am totally guaranteed one as have lovely boyfriend.

Wednesday 14
Valentine's Day

10 a.m.
No card. It is obviously delayed in Britain's notoriously haphazard postal system. Or else is being delivered by hand later at our romantic dinner (i.e. Luigi's Pizza). But, controversially, one has arrived for Dad and it is not from Mum (hers was on the table with his Shreddies this morning, plus she would not buy anything with a pink pearlized envelope, or squirt it with Poison). Mum is beside herself with potential love rivalry. James has suggested steaming it open with the kettle. But I said this broke all sorts of trust issues and she should respect Dad's right to privacy.

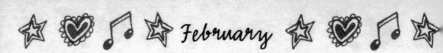

10.15 a.m.
Mum is steaming open the card with the kettle. God, hope it is not from Edie but from random stalker, or actually for James by mistake (not completely out of the question, as he has eight this year, a new record. It is due to his high ranking as a gang member.)

10.30 a.m.
Card is from Edie (she signed it 'your Weirdy Edie' followed by seven kisses). Mum is threatening to go round to Mr Wilmott's and have it out with her (do not rate Edie's chances—she is in a weakened state due to alcohol withdrawal and Mum is nutritionally tip-top, thanks to fruit muesli and granary toast.) Have called Dad to warn him. He is coming home immediately. Which means there is a definite crisis looming. He did not even take time off when Mum had gastroenteritis and James had to cook his tea (I was banned from cooking at time due to my inability to follow recipes or keep ingredients off floor).

12 noon
Dad is back and has gone straight into the talks suite (i.e. the dining room). James is positioned at door with an upturned glass (Mum would ban *Blue Peter* if she knew that was where he had learned this trick).

12.05 p.m.
Dad has called Mum a 'meddler' for opening his post.

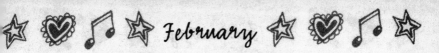

12.10 p.m.
Mum has accused Dad of being a philanderer for receiving said post.

12.15 p.m.
Dad is out and is demanding to see evidence of said philandering post.

12.30 p.m.
Evidence not located. Dad accuses Mum of fabricating evidence.

12.45 p.m.
Dog is sick (pink pearlized, scent of Poison) outside back door. Mum points to sick and says, 'Read that and weep, Colin Riley.'

1 p.m.
Colin Riley declines to read sick but declares he has no interest in Edie, that she is clutching at straws following their brief liaison in 1982 and that, as everyone knows, high school love affairs are meaningless and fizzle out after a few years unless you are blessed with the imagination of a newt (or Clive and Marjory) and it is university ones that go the distance (he met Mum at accountancy college). Mum agrees, following statistical evidence produced by James and his trusty companion, Google. (Justin and I will be the exception to this rule, obviously.)

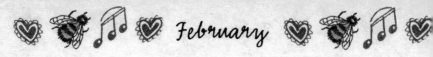

1.15 p.m.

Peace is restored and Dad returns to work with cottage cheese sandwich, prepared by loving wife. Sick is cleaned up and flushed away, along with evidence of Edie's undying passion for Sex Beast Riley.

Thank God crisis is over. Am going to have to raise the issue with Tuesday though. Will tell her she needs to rein in her mother's urges, or she will be possibly responsible for putting me into care and thus ruining my chances of passing my GCSEs and being generally brilliant.

5 p.m.

Am meeting Justin in an hour at our assignation point (i.e. Barry Island for pre-meal snogging). Am going to wear floaty scarf (as worn by model types at Glastonbury, although this is one of Mum's 1970s M&S cast-offs, not genuine Pucci). Scarf looks very vintage plus will disguise lack of activity in breast area. (James's idea.) Think tonight may be the night, i.e. when Justin declares his love for me. Scarlet says Trevor 'pledged his troth' on Friday 13th—a special goth day (the Stones do not celebrate Valentine's Day, due to it being overcommercial and possibly made up by chocolate manufacturers). Mum says I must be home by ten or she will come and collect me herself in the Fiesta. Will be home by 9.30. Do not want Mum ruining mood of love with her current anti-romance stance, or her usual carping on about the lack of food hygiene on the help yourself salad bar or the rogue apostrophes on the menu.

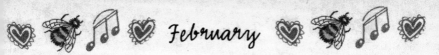

9.30 p.m.

Am back from romantic dinner i.e. ham and pineapple pizza and all-you-can-eat ice cream factory. Result—no declaration of love but some excellent across table snogging. Asked him about card. He said I was right, it is trapped in the woeful Royal Mail. (I may well write to Trade Secretary to complain – he is thwarting love lives up and down the country. Especially as it is bound to be literary and tragic with seventeenth century paintings of lovestruck beauty on it. Unlike Edie's whimsical puppies effort.) Then floaty scarf thing caught fire on the Valentine's candles and Justin threw glass of 7Up at me to quash flames i.e. save my life. Am definitely in love. Stomach feels all gurgly with excitement. Justin is the ONE after all. Hurrah.

2 a.m.

Have been sick. It is nerves from love-fuelled dinner.

2.30 a.m.

Oh. And again.

3.00 a.m.

More sick. Maybe it is not nerves, but Hawaiian pizza. Or Mr Whippy style chemical ice cream.

3.30 a.m.

Sick definitely fault of Luigi. Have just got text from Justin cancelling our romantic lunch (baguettes from Pie Shop

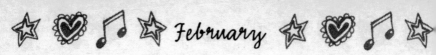
Pearce) as he is locked in his Tudor-style toilet on Debden Road also being sick.

Thursday 15

4 p.m.
Still feeling ill. Mum has called Uttlesford Environmental Health (i.e. Mrs O'Nion aka Mrs Onion) to demand Luigi's Pizza is shut down immediately on grounds of salmonella and false advertising (Luigi is actually called Dave and is from Sible Hedingham, not Napoli). Mrs O'Nion says she needs proof, i.e. a vomit sample. Mum is now hovering with a bucket in the hope I produce some more.

Justin is too weak to visit. He has lost half a stone in six hours. Sad Ed was not too weak to visit (he could do with getting food poisoning—may suggest it as a diet tip). He had brought a Get Well Mix CD of 'soothing' New Wave Indie pop. Had to ask him to turn it off after a while as the twangy guitars and tuneless lyrics were causing new waves of nausea. Told him about the Edie crisis. He says he will mention it to Tuesday but that Edie is on a knife edge at the moment and rejection could send her straight back into the arms of Jack Daniels and Johnny Walker. I said I did not care who else she snogged as long as it is not vest-wearing Colin Riley.

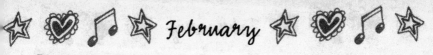
Friday 16

Am still weak from pizza poisoning. Mum is not best pleased though as have failed to produce more vomit for her forensic sample. I said she should be relieved I am on the mend. She said on the contrary, what would make her happy is shutting down Luigi's rat-infested kitchens. Have called Scarlet to cancel planned shopping pilgrimage to Cambridge with Suzy for Converse footwear and Topshop skinny jeans. She is going to take Trevor instead as he wants to buy some black nail varnish from the big Boots. Have texted Justin but he says he is still sipping Lucozade in a darkened room and does not want to walk the fifteen minutes from his Tudor-style mansion to no-apparent-style Summerdale Road in case he collapses. I texted back to say it was very rock star to collapse on a pavement. He said yes but from alcohol poisoning, not crap pizza.

4 p.m.
Got text from Jack—HP U BETTER. NEED ANYTHING? MAGAZINES? GRAPES? WIPES? Texted back saying thanks but that I had full supply of fruit and mopping up equipment and that I needed nothing.

Oooh. Although maybe a magazine would be nice. Maybe should text back and ask him to come over. Oh he has texted back already.

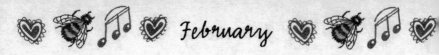
4.10 p.m.

It says SUIT YOURSELF RILEY. He is so moody. Maybe he has boy PMT. Rosamund says it is entirely possibly due to excess oestrogen in the water supply (pill-taking people weeing). She only drinks bottled Evian and fresh rainwater. Or else it is nerves because of inaugural Jack Stone Five gig tomorrow.

Saturday 17

8 a.m.

Ugh. Work. Was going to phone in sick (almost genuine) but Mum says there is no way I am going out tonight to get sweaty with a load of rampaging teenagers if I am too ill to price up Fruesli bars first. Plus she is refusing to pay £3.50 for the ticket so I need to earn my entrance fee. James is backing her strong work ethic. He has amassed £4.00 this week by washing the Fiesta, spring cleaning the frog tank, cutting the dog's toenails, and learning the Latin names for garden birds. I said I didn't get paid to be clever and maybe I should get money for passing my GCSEs. Mum said my reward would be the joy of knowing I have worked hard to improve my career chances. I said I'd rather have £10 an exam. Then James demanded £10 for every spelling test he passes and at that point Mum told us to stop the money madness and eat our Shreddies.

Am taking gig outfit to work so I can get changed at

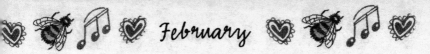

Justin's. All the members of 'Pigeon' (as it is now known because we are all bored with the full length version) are meeting there so we can go in as one and show our solidarity. Except for Sad Ed who is on late trolley duty and will have to walk to the ATC hut in his brown overall. Justin is very excited. He thinks he will be like Nigel Tuffnell in Spinal Tap and that Jack will see him in the audience and be overwhelmed with regret and call him on stage for a Certain Death reunion. I said he should not care about his old band and that Pigeon is the future of music in North Essex. He said The Death will always be Number One in his eyes.

12 midnight

Justin did not get called on stage for a reunion. Even more depressingly, the Jack Stone Five are excellent. Tuesday is totally Lily Allenish and did songs about the cars at Barry Island and drinking coffee at the new Starbucks (formerly the White Horse, spiritual home of Treena). Although I think their version of 'LDN' ('WLDN') was pushing it a bit. I can think of a million reasons why I would want to be anywhere else than Saffron Walden, sun in the sky or not. Worse, Jack looked really good on drums and smiled at me loads. Unlike Justin who leant moodily against the wall with a Fanta and refused to talk to anyone.

Walked home with Sad Ed and Tuesday as Justin said he was too down to snog. Tuesday was on a complete high. She says she is single-handedly breaking down the barriers of

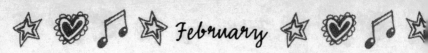

February

apartheid that separate the Quakers and John Major High with the power of her voice, and likened herself to Nelson Mandela. I said I was not sure he would look so favourably on the comparison but Tuesday said I was just jealous because I am behind the scenes and she is in the limelight. It is the story of my life.

On the plus side, Tuesday said she has told Edie not to send Dad any more love letters. Edie said she would try, but that he is like an addiction and she may not be strong enough to fight it. I said she had better be or she would have Mum to deal with, which will be worse than going cold turkey from the Smirnoff.

Sunday 18

Justin is fully revived and I have the lovebite to prove it (concealed with floaty scarf before Mum sends me to borstal)! He says he is not taking the Jack Stone Five's success lying down and we are going to come back bigger and better. He has instructed me to book the ATC hut for Friday 2nd March. Rehearsals start in earnest after school on Wednesday. Hurrah. It is because he went home and watched *The Doors* starring the crap Batman and realized he IS Jim Morrison. I said Sad Ed claims HE is Jim Morrison too but Justin says he has the wrong hair and that Sad Ed is actually Ray Manzarek. Anyway, he is banishing Sad Ed's crap guitar and is making him learn the

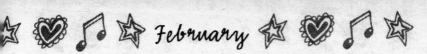

synthesizer immediately. He is going round later with his Bontempi organ. He says he will upgrade it for a Yamaha when we have sold out our first tour. He may be waiting a long time.

7 p.m.

Went round Sad Ed's to see how he was taking the news of his new role but could hear 'Chopsticks' being played badly out of bedroom window on the Bontempi so decided to leave him to his music. Plus have school tomorrow and need to mentally prepare for tough GCSE teaching schedule.

Monday 19

Did not have tough GCSE teaching schedule. Instead got sent home with a fake baby. It is for Citizenship and we are supposed to work out when it needs feeding and nappy changing and not dropping on its head etc. We have all got one, except Emily Reeve who will have a real one to not drop on its head in six months' time. Plus Ms Hopwood-White said it is pointless as the idea is to terrify us into not getting pregnant and it would be like shutting the stable door after the horse has bolted. I have called mine Desdemona (after tragic Shakespearean heroine). She is resting peacefully on the sofa. Will obviously make an excellent mother, once have conquered literary world.

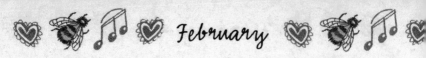
Also tried to befriend Emily Reeve in attempt to gain her confidence so she can confess who the father is etc., but she asked me to go away as I was eating trail mix (replacing Maltesers in Mr Wilmott's new-style vending machine) and the peanut particles could kill her and her unborn child. She is so ungrateful. If I were in her position I would be taking up all offers of friendship I could get.

5 p.m.
Have fed Desdemona and changed nappy (i.e. pressed appropriate buttons on control panel). She has not cried once. Hurrah. Am obviously a natural at this. I bet things are not so peaceful in the Sad Ed household. He will have killed his for sure already with his fat fingers.

8 p.m.
Desdemona is crying incessantly. Which is very annoying as am trying to watch television but Mum has banished me from the room as she can't hear Bill Oddy above the wailing. Will feed her again.

9 p.m.
And again.

10 p.m.
And again. How can she still be hungry? She is worse than the dog.

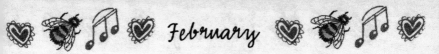
2 a.m.

Aagh. Desdemona still crying. Have fed her and changed her but she will not shut up. Have locked her in shed. Ms Hopwood-White will never know.

Tuesday 20
Shrove Tuesday (i.e. Pancake Day)

Ms Hopwood White says I have killed Desdemona with neglect. I said she was malfunctioning and overdemanding food. Ms Hopwood-White said, *au contraire*, I had overfed her and given her chronic colic. Did not tell her about shed. She has reset her and says I can have another go. In stark contrast the Kylies have highly contented fake babies (Dolshay and Jordan-Jade). It is because they have the unfair advantage of getting to practise on all the many mini O'Gradys.

4 p.m.

Mum is not allowing Desdemona back into the house. Apparently Marjory came over at breakfast convinced that murderous urban foxes were digging a lair in the shed last night. Anyway it does not matter. I have had a genius idea. Am going to get Treena to look after Desdemona. She has to get up for Jesus anyway so one more baby will be no bother at all.

6 p.m.

Desdemona dead again (fatal blow to head). Treena killed

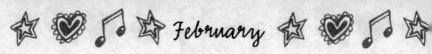

her within an hour. This does not bode well for Jesus's future. Have reset her and brought her home. Will just have to try harder not to overfeed this time. Mum says one bout of colic and she is a goner.

10 p.m.
Desdemona fed and changed. All is quiet. Have definitely got hang of it all.

Wednesday 21
Ash Wednesday

7 a.m.
Have had excellent peaceful night and Desdemona slept all the way through, which is more than I can say for the dog who was making a racket in the living room at 4 a.m. Maybe I will become a child-rearing genius like that Gina Ford person. I will patent my method and make a fortune.

7.15 a.m.
Oh God. Dog has killed Desdemona. She is not just dead, but viciously hacked in several pieces. And one arm is missing, presumed eaten. Am going to fail Citizenship. And possibly be banned from ever having children (by Mum, not school, she has far more jurisdiction in these matters). Maybe will leave remains at home and say she is doing so well would like to keep her until end of week. Yes, will do

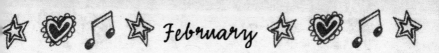

that. And in meantime can purchase talking Tiny Tears as replacement.

6 p.m.
Ms Hopwood-White agreed that I can keep Desdemona until Friday. She says she is glad I am taking the challenge so seriously and I am an inspiration to the rest of the class (bulk of babies dead, including Scarlet's fake son Frankenstein who got killed when she tried to give him a gothic baptism in a bath of blood (red food colouring)). Only survivor is Jordan-Jade. Fat Kylie is now thinking of becoming a nursery nurse.

Band practice was very exciting. The new sound is a definite improvement. Justin is sexier than ever in his ripped shirt and beads. And Sad Ed has learned 'Baa Baa Black Sheep' and the theme tune to *EastEnders* in the space of three days. He says he will have 'Light My Fire' off by heart by the gig. Also we have a new name. We are The Back Doors in homage to the mighty Jim.

10 p.m.
Oops. Have to book gig. Will do so after school tomorrow.

Thursday 22

Hurrah. Valentine's Day card has arrived. Admittedly it is eight days late and is novelty rude one with unrepeatable

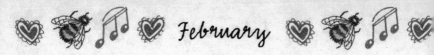

joke inside, as opposed to previously imagined portrait of star-crossed lovers. But is a card none the less and further proof of Justin's undying love for me. Plus, it escaped Mum's rigorous taste checks (it would have failed for sure due to inclusion of word pussy, possibly not in a cat context). She is not having a sudden progressive streak. She is preoccupied due to her and Dad having a Bupa medical check today. Dad looks nervous. He thinks they may find out he is riddled with life-threatening conditions. In contrast Mum is not scared. She welcomes exams of any kind and says she will pass with flying colours.

Scarlet is outraged though. She says private healthcare is the province of the 'chattering classes' (which is rich as Suzy excels at chattering), is anti-Labour and a blow to left-wing radicalism everywhere. She says it is creating a two-tier health service where the rich can pay to have their cholesterol-clogged arteries swooshed out or whatever it is they do and the poor have to wait on trolleys in their own wee. I said Dad got it free at work and that she was being un-Labour by highlighting trolleys, waiting lists, and dirty hospitals. She went white. She has never been accused of being un-Labour before and had to immediately reconnect with her left-wing roots by reading *Das Capital* under the table in Maths.

5 p.m.

Mum and Dad are back from their Bupa check and, in a shock move, have both been given stern cholesterol warnings. Mum is livid. She is blaming Granny Clegg for

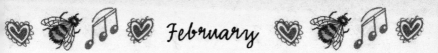

feeding her Fray Bentos and beef dripping in her formative years. Dad on the other hand is jubilant that he is not alone in his battle against the bulge. But his happiness was short-lived because Mum imposed an immediate embargo on all dairy products and has driven to Waitrose on an emergency skimmed soya milk and Benecol mission.

Friday 23

Had skimmed soya milk on my Shreddies at breakfast. It is vile and tastes of liquid cardboard. Threw it away and tried Marmite and Benecol on toast. Also unsatisfactory. Worse, Mum wants to invite Justin for tea after work on Saturday. He is going to chuck me for sure if she makes him eat her new cholesterol-free fayre.

And have failed to purchase talking Tiny Tears to replace Desdemona so James has glued the original back with some Copydex. Am worried Ms Hopwood-White might spot teeth marks and constant tinny whirring noise. Also doll is still one arm down. It is lodged somewhere inside dog's vast intestinal system, along with the Duplo and two AA batteries.

4 p.m.
Ms Hopwood-White says she has never seen such an abused child and if this was a real situation I would be on my way to prison. I said if it was real, I would not have left Desdemona in the fridge for the night (soundproofed), from whence

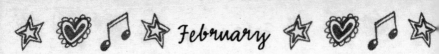
the dog snatched her while it was looking for cold ham. She said I should hope not, and gave me a bill for £100 to replace the baby. That is a lot of money for a doll. Treena would sell Jesus for that sort of money.

Also, asked Justin to 'meet the parents'. He says is there any way of not coming. I said not really, or he was risking a permanent ban. He is worried my dad will be like Robert de Niro and menace him with his overprotective ways. It is not Dad he should be worried about. He will just nod at appropriate moments and go back to watching golf. It is Mum who will be using CIA-like tactics to catch him out.

5 p.m.
Mum says the Desdemona bill is the last straw. She is ringing Grandpa tomorrow to collect the dog. I said she was condemning it to a life of misery on Harvey Road, and it may get chewed to death by Fat Kylie's poodle Tupac or forced to take part in an illegal dog baiting ring, but Mum said it should have thought of that before. James said she had a heart of stone but then she threatened to exile Michaelangelo and Donatello as well so he went upstairs to do anti-Shredder training with the frogs.

Saturday 24

Am very nervous about *Meet the Parents*-style high tea. Have begged Mum to supply éclairs and Duchy chocolate

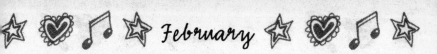
things but she says she cannot trust Dad to stay away from cholesterol-laden goods and is going to bake a no-fat courgette cake, as detailed in *Good Housekeeping*. James is helping her. He is in charge of weights and measures, as he is meticulous in these areas. But maybe it will not be disastrous. Maybe he will think they are slightly bohemian and new-wave and will love me even more.

7 p.m.
Meet the Parents tea was disastrous. Courgette cake was like eating moist savoury flannels. 'Entertainment' was supplied by James who decided to seize the moment to sing the books of the Bible song. Plus Mum wore support tights which are decidedly unbohemian. Worse, Justin cracked after only ten minutes of Paxmanesque grilling and confessed to once passively inhaling the smoke from a joint at which point Mum's lips went so thin they disappeared and I could tell she was planning to rework her anti-drugs lecture. It is lucky he did not confess that said joint actually belonged to Suzy or I would be banned from Scarlet's for ever more. In the end Dad offered to give him a lift home. I think he was glad to escape the fraught fat-free atmosphere as well.

On the plus side, the dog has gone. So I can abandon Resolution 6 to train it. The house is now a hair-free and pest-free zone. Although the frogs are still vile. And they are showing no signs of being magic Ninja frogs either. They just float aimlessly around their tank eating mince.

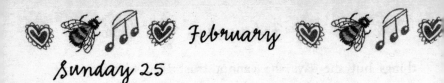

Sunday 25

Went to band practice. Justin still slightly dazed from yesterday's interrogation. I said he will get used to it. He said, 'Yeah, maybe.' Not sure what that means. The Back Doors sounded quite good though. God, still have not booked gig. Am crap manager. Will do it in morning behind bike sheds (i.e. smokers' and illegal mobile phoners' corner).

Monday 26

Oh my God. Scarlet says she is thinking of chucking Trevor. Apparently he is not happy about her move towards EMO (as predicted by me, Rachel Riley) and is questioning her commitment to the dark side. It is the new skinny jeans and the non-regulation Converse (i.e. they are pink as opposed to goth-approved black). Scarlet says he is trying to control her identity, which is the first sign of domestic abuse. I said Trevor didn't look much like a wife beater but she says it is the quiet ones you have to watch out for. And the weedy bat-like ones apparently. She is going to give it a week to see if his attitude improves.

Tuesday 27

Mum has just reminded us it is Dad's birthday tomorrow.

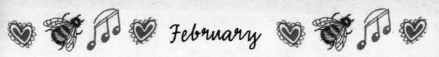

Have to get card and present after school. Will get Justin to come with me. He will know what men like. James has already purchased his gift. It is a giant staple gun.

5 p.m.
Have bought Dad the *Carol's Best of Countdown* on DVD. Justin says all old men like Carol Vorderman, it is genetic. It is true. She is Dad's favourite intellectual TV presenter.

Wednesday 28

Dad's birthday. Gave Dad his *Countdown* DVD. Mum failed to make 'oh what a nice idea' comments which accompanied opening of giant stapler though. She is obviously still reeling from the Edie/Sex Beast thing and worried intellectual Carol may fan the flames of desire with her short leather skirts and conundrum-solving skills.

5 p.m.
Dad's stapler has been quarantined. James has stapled all his socks to the wall. He says it is modern art but Mum does not agree.

I'm RACHEL RILEY
— welcome to my so-called life.

March

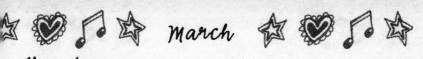

March

Thursday 1
St David's Day (Wales)

Had final band practice before tomorrow's debut gig and had awful realization that have utterly failed to book venue. Asked Justin if he thought maybe we should delay a bit, given our fledgling new sound, but he said it is too late, the posters are up in the common room and he has already sold seven tickets. Am too ashamed to admit truth to Justin so am just going to turn up and hope for the best. It is bound to be unlocked as the Brownies will have been in there for toadstool jumping etc. after school.

Friday 2

6 p.m.
Thank God. Brownies were still in there doing semaphore when we arrived. Roadies (i.e. me and three Year Sevens who are trying to gain access to the Alternative Music Club table) have set up equipment and sound check is now under way. It is very exciting as the hordes will be arriving in less than two hours.

7.30 p.m.
No sign of hordes as yet. So far audience is Justin's mum and dad, Stan's mum and dad, the surprisingly tall Dwarf family, the roadies, and Tuesday (Sad Ed's parents do not

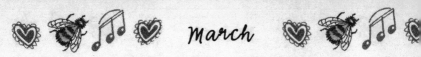

believe in music unless it is Welsh and religious i.e. Aled Jones). Am sure it will be busy by the time The Back Doors take the stage, i.e. in thirty minutes, and the gig will be legendary, like the Beatles at the Cavern Club, or Blind Mice at Hadstock Village Hall.

10 p.m.

The gig was legendary, but not in a good way. The only hordes to arrive were the ATC who had been out practising machete skills on the fields behind the recycling centre (aka the dump) and were expecting a talk on semi-automatic weaponry. Tried to broker peaceful deal whereby they could look at pictures of guns in the car park while the gig finished but forgot that ATC membership includes Mark Lambert, Mr Whippy, and several O'Gradys. Plus at crucial moment, Justin cued the band in for their version of 'People are Strange', which the ATC took as deliberate provocation and seized their chance to attack. Scarlet showed up with Jack and Trevor just as Dean the Dwarf got hurled into the disabled toilet. Jack just said, 'Great gig, Riley,' and walked out again. On the plus side, Scarlet got caught in the crossfire and Trevor nursed her tenderly under his giant bat cloak so he is in her good books for the moment. I, on the other hand, have been sacked. Justin says it is a purely business decision and is nothing to do with our personal relationship. But it is a bad sign. Plus breasts still barely discernible. I have no chance.

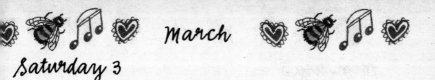

Saturday 3

Work. Justin seemed distinctly distracted during our lunchtime meat bin snogging. I asked if he had found a new band manager yet and he said he had someone in mind. Oh God. What if it is Sophie Microwave Muffins? Her dad can get free cake mix and logo T-shirts after all. What can I offer? Health-giving snacks and James's fabric paints. There is no contest. I have to do something excellent and Simon Cowell-like to win back his trust or risk losing him to an older woman. With 34C breasts.

Sunday 4

A strange man keeps walking past the house. He is wearing a balaclava, several tattoos, and a distinctly menacing look. James has catalogued him in Mum's anti-social behaviour notebook (Mum was otherwise engaged with Jesus and her flashcards—we are baby- and pet-sitting while Grandpa and Treena enjoy some quality time together, i.e. having sex and watching Sky). I pointed out that you couldn't report someone for walking but James said he has done it twenty-seven times, which constitutes persistent lurking and/or potential obsessive compulsive disorder. Tried to get the dog to go out and scare him away but he was too busy watching Noel Edmonds.

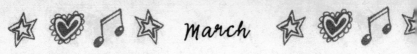

Monday 5

The menacing man was back again after school. He sat on Thin Kylie's wall pretending to read *Vogue*. Maybe he is a gay burglar casing us for weaknesses in our security arrangements. He will be sorely disappointed. Mum has fitted two different kinds of window lock and has a sawn off hoe by the back door for bludgeoning miscreants. Plus Marjory has eyes like a hawk. She once spotted Sad Ed performing an illegal wheelie two roads away.

Tuesday 6

No menacing burglar today. It is highly disappointing. I was quite enjoying having a potential madman lurking about. It makes a change from watching Terry and Cherie picking fag ends up from the lawn in their woefully revealing dressing gowns.

School utterly boring. Except for Rural Studies and that was only because we got to round up goats. It was not for GCSE, it was because Mark Lambert and Davey MacDonald had sneaked them out at lunch for an illegal goat race and the goats, unsurprisingly, had not stuck to the track but had veered off towards the gates and their ultimate freedom.

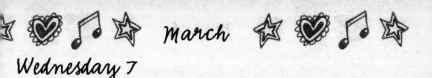
Wednesday 7

Hurrah, menacing man back this afternoon. Reading *New Woman* this time. He is surprisingly eclectic in his reading tastes for a burglar.

Also, Mum has found evidence of illicit chocolate eating on Dad's work clothes. She says there is Twix caramel congealed in his jacket pocket. Dad is denying it but Mum says there is no mistaking its claggy consistency. She is threatening to perform random swoops at Wainwright and Hogg.

Thursday 8

I have found my Golden Ticket back to music impresarioness (not entirely sure that is a word but cannot think of right one), and, more importantly, to Justin's heart. The *Walden Chronicle* has declared a Battle of the Bands! It says:

> **Are you the next Antarctic Monkeys?**

(Answer—possibly, although this band is clearly made up due to ace reporter Glen Davies's utter lack of musical knowledge.)

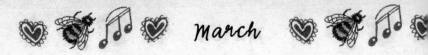
> Does your drummer have more rhythm than Phil Collins?

(Answer—no, but he is marginally less freaky looking despite being a dwarf.)

> Then the Walden Chronicle needs you! WHERE?—Lord Butler Leisure Centre, Jockey Wilson Suite

(i.e. not Wembley but a step up from the ATC hut.)

> WHEN—Saturday 28 April. Be there or be square!

Best of all, one of the judges is newspaper editor (and wife of owner) Deirdre Roberts, my former work experience supervisor. So I have connections to the judges and may be able to sway their vital decision. Hurrah! Obviously I will not use underhand methods to purchase success (as have no means of doing so even if wanted to, am still paying off £100 doll bill with Nuts In May wages) but will merely point out The Back Doors' potential for world domination. Now just have to persuade Justin to enter, persuade him to take me back as manager, and persuade Deirdre to meet for musical discussions.

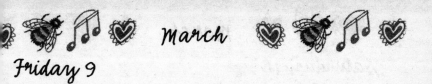

Friday 9

9 a.m.
Tackled Justin about the Battle of the Bands and my imminent reinstatement as manager outside Mr Patel's before school. He said he is not entering 'amateur hour' because the competition is likely to be a bunch of ten year olds on recorders (possibly true—James is at this very moment trying to persuade Reverend Begley to let him form a chime bar duo with Mad Harry).

10.20 a.m.
The Back Doors are in the Battle of the Bands after all. It is because the Jack Stone Five have already posted their entry form and £5 fee to Deirdre. Justin says there is no way he is letting that bandwagon-jumping Brit Pop pretty boy steal his thunder. He says rock will rule, and The Back Doors will conquer Saffron Walden, and then, who knows? Sad Ed said Harlow. But I think it was meant to be rhetorical because Justin rolled his eyes and went off to practise catching peanuts in his mouth (he is second best in the lower sixth, after Whitey Wilson (albino, but with unfair advantage of oversize mouth)).

Also, he says he will be making a management announcement at band practice tomorrow. This does not bode well. What if it is Sophie Microwave Muffins? She might forbid him to have a girlfriend in case it interferes with his music. And then he will be at her total mercy.

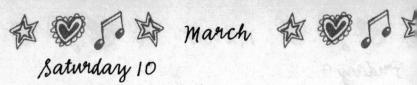
Saturday 10

Could not concentrate on my work (i.e. sweeping up rogue lentils) due to Sophie Microwave Muffins management turmoil. Had to abandon lunch in favour of emergency mission to the Waitrose trolley park to discuss crisis with Sad Ed. He said I am worrying about nothing. There is no way Justin would let Sophie manage the band as she has no understanding of rock, i.e. she went to see Girls Aloud on tour. He said the manager will be someone who has cavernous musical knowledge and an appreciation of the technical side of band management. Which is totally me! I am excellent at plugging in amps.

Sunday 11

The new manager is not Sophie. Or me. It is Sad Ed! He is a total traitor and has been pestering Justin for weeks apparently. I demanded an immediate vote. But Justin said I should not put myself through the inevitable humiliation. I said I was not afraid of the opinion of the people i.e. the band. So we had a vote. I lost by two to one. (Only The Dwarf stood by me in my hour of need.) I pointed out Sad Ed's poor track record on organizing large-scale events (his tenth birthday party had an attendance of three—me, him, and Scarlet) but Justin said it is just better to keep these things in the band. I said it was jobs for the boys but Justin

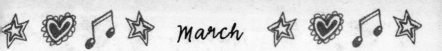
said there are plenty of jobs for the girls, like chief groupie. Asked what this involved. Basically I have to snog Justin. Which I do already. But if he is busy, he can pass me on to another band member. I said this was utterly anti-feminist but he said *au contraire*, it is utterly liberating. So said yes. Hope do not have to snog The Dwarf though. He will have to stand on a box. Or I would have to kneel. Which is just weird.

Monday 12
Commonwealth Day

Asked Scarlet if she wanted to be second groupie for the Back Doors. She said she would rather chew tinfoil than prostitute herself to a bunch of semi-talented schoolboys, especially as one of them is Sad Ed. I said it was utterly not prostitution but very liberal, which she is all in favour of. But she has a better idea. We are going to form a girl band and beat the boys at their own game! Admittedly, there are only two of us, and we can play no instruments at all other than the recorder, but, even so, it is an excellent plan. Scarlet says we will be like Janis Joplin and Joni Mitchell. I agreed, even though have no idea who these people are. She is bound to be right—she has the advantage of Suzy's vast musical (and sexual) knowledge. Scarlet is going to learn the guitar in record time and I am going to be chief lyricist i.e. write some songs, as I am potentially excellent poet type.

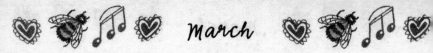

We already have a name—it is Velvet Elvis. Am glad I did not waste it on Justin now! Cannot wait to tell him about our band. Now we are totally like Kurt and Courtney as we are both musical geniuses.

5 p.m.
Justin not quite as embracing of my musical career as had hoped. In fact, he begged me not to go on stage and sing. He says he is just worried I will not be able to handle the cut-throat world that is the music business. But it is probably fear that I will outshine him musically. Anyway, have resigned as first groupie and said we must keep our snogging on a strictly non-business arrangement.

6 p.m.
But what if he gives job to someone else, i.e. Miss Nipples Pervert Jacobs? Will ring him immediately and demand reinstatement.

6.15 p.m.
Am groupie and girl band member. That way I am not closing off any options, should one career falter.

Tuesday 13

Treena rang. Jesus has taken his first steps. Treena has been luring him using a trail of Cheetos. Asked if he could walk

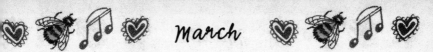

on water (as a joke) but Treena obviously has not read the Bible, as she said she didn't know and would try immediately. Oh God. Hope she is not going to get him to stride across the Slade. He will drown in the trolley-infested waters, or get bitten by a rat.

5 p.m.
Jesus cannot walk on water. He sank to bottom of bath, injuring Grandpa Riley who was submerged in Radox at time. Both are now being revived with hot towels and Wagon Wheels.

Wednesday 14

James has offered to be in the band. It is because Reverend Begley has refused him and Mad Harry permission to form a chime bar duo. (I do not blame him. The chime bars would never be the same again.) I have also said no, on the grounds that he is a boy and we are strictly a girl band. Plus he can only play crap instruments (i.e. chime bars and triangle).

Thursday 15

Wrote a song during Rural Studies. (Was supposed to be learning about yoghurt-making but when will I need that

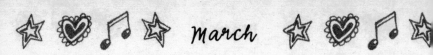

march

skill? That is what Waitrose is for.) It is called 'Bad Bat Boy and the Skinny Jeans' and is all about Trevor and Scarlet and their relationship issues. It is essential to take inspiration from real life. Although have not used actual names so Trevor will never know it is about him.

I have two verses and a chorus so far:

Bad Bat Boy and the Skinny Jeans
Your eyes are red (contact lenses—not blood),
Your clothes are black,

You've got a pair of wings (this is true—
they are black net ones, made by his mum),
You wear a floor-length leather coat,
And twenty-seven rings.

But you don't love my skinny jeans,
Yeah, you don't love my skinny jeans,
Yeah, you don't love my skinny jeans,
So you just don't love me.

Your hair is long with purple streaks,
You have a cage of rats,
But secretly you really wish,
That it was legal to keep bats.

Chorus etc.

Scarlet says it is excellent. She is going to write some music in Citizenship then we are going to jam at hers on Saturday.

Friday 16

James's pedantry has reached new levels. He has written to Mr Patel to complain about the bubble gum machine outside, which claims its contents 'taste like your favourite fruit'. Apparently Keanu got some and it did not taste like his favourite fruit at all (i.e. banana). James has taken on his cause. I admire the way he is fighting with his intellect, rather than his fists. Maybe he will inspire Keanu to give up his life of violence.

Saturday 17
St Patrick's Day

Hurrah. Am going over to Scarlet's after work for band practice. Told Justin during lunch (past sell-by-date sausage rolls). He said he hoped I was not going to put my music career before my love life. I said on the contrary I would stop by for a snog after *Casualty*.

9 p.m.
Band practice was promising. Scarlet is better at guitar than Sad Ed already. Suzy says she has inherited her talents from

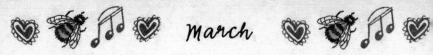

March

her. (She did the background clapping and swaying in a David Bowie video once.) Jack came to watch us do 'Bad Bat Boy and the Skinny Jeans' (it is our only song so we did it eleven times). He said, 'Not bad, Riley. Maybe we could work on one for the Jack Stone Five.' I said no chance, it would be like Gary Barlow writing a song for Westlife. He said, 'Whatever,' and went back to his blackened room to philosophize. Or possibly read *Nuts* magazine. (Justin's current favourite. He says it is not the semi-naked women he likes, it is the book reviews. Which is possibly true. Loads of famous writer types have been published in *Playboy* after all.)

Went round Justin's after *Casualty* for prearranged snog. He asked how it had gone. I said excellently and that even Jack was impressed. Then Justin got all annoyed and said he had to go and practise moody rock looks in the mirror. He is obviously still funny about Jack after the wardrobe snog confusion. He has nothing to fear. I do not love Jack. Although it is quite nice that he is jealous. It is because I am utterly vintage and lovely.

10 p.m.
Or maybe it is Jack that he is sad about. Maybe it is like *Brokeback Mountain* and actually he wishes it was like before when they hung out together and played guitar and did man things. Ooh. And I am like the glamorous rodeo girl i.e. American beauty Anne Hathaway.

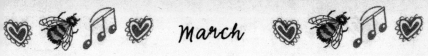

10.15 p.m.
Or maybe I am dowdy one with too many babies who gets all shouty and marries the grocer.

Sunday 18
Mothering Sunday (i.e. Mother's Day)

8 a.m.
James and I are up and are going to make Mum breakfast in bed. We are doing scrambled eggs and bacon.

8.30 a.m.
Breakfast in bed cancelled due to Mum refusing to stay in bed during breakfast making. Apparently the fear of egg spillage (and potential cholesterol ingestion) was giving her hives and so Dad sent her down to put her mind at rest. Made relatively risk-free Marmite on toast instead.

10 a.m.
Menacing man is back. He is watching Dad wash the car from behind *Grazia*. Mum has called 999 but Tracey Hughes's mum who answers the phones got quite annoyed with her and said she could be prosecuted for wasting police time. So she said, 'Why, what are they doing that is so important, walking the Alsatians round Waitrose car park?' Obviously this is exactly what they were doing, as she quickly agreed to send a patrol car round to investigate. Mum said it had better be sharpish

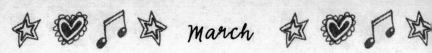
in case the menacing man is armed, or bipolar, or both, and attacks. She has made Dad come back in as a safety precaution.

11 a.m.
No sign of patrol car. Menacing man still looking at pictures of celebrity cellulite.

12 noon
No patrol car.

1 p.m.
Menacing man finishes *Grazia* and moves on. Possibly to purchase *Heat*.

3 p.m.
Patrol car arrives. Mum goes out to read riot act to PC Doone. He apologizes but they had a last-minute call out to a brawl in Tesco's condiments aisle. It is bound to be an O'Grady. Or possibly several. Mum said it will be on his head when the menacing man goes bonkers with a Colt 45 (Mum only knows guns from Westerns due to Grandpa Clegg's John Wayne fascination) and showers shoppers with bullets. Then I distinctly heard PC Doone mutter that Mum is a paranoid fantasist (possibly true), but luckily, the frogs chose that moment to get stuck in a soggy Smarties tube (James was trying to acclimatize them to the sewer) and Mum had to go upstairs to release them (liquid soap and a good poke with a toothbrush).

Monday 19

Granny Clegg rang to report that her hip of doom had been right all along. According to Maureen Penrice in Spar, Denzil, as in Denzil's Crazy Car Warehouse in Camborne, choked to death on a sherbet lemon at the weekend. Mum pointed out the several-week gap between the hip pains and ensuing death but Granny Clegg says the fateful sherbet lemons were purchased from Maureen the very day her hip had started playing up. Then Mum got annoyed with the whole magic hip thing and told her she should call up the Home Office as her hip could play a vital role in murder prevention. But now she is in a panic as Granny Clegg does not understand sarcasm and is bound to actually do it.

Tuesday 20

Granny Clegg has rung again. Apparently Devon and Cornwall Constabulary are strangely uninterested in her potential crime-solving hip. She says they are mad and that her hip could be their very own Miss Marple. She is thinking of offering its services to the Russians instead, just to spite them. (The Cleggs think we are still locked in cold war conflict with the Communists. They also think the iron curtain is an actual iron curtain. Dad asked them where it was once. Grandpa Clegg said somewhere in Poland.)

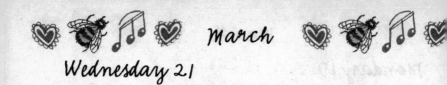

March

Wednesday 21

The hip of doom is hurting again. Granny Clegg has phoned the police but they have told her to call Dr Kimber or rub it with Deep Heat. Mum is with the police but Granny says we will all be sorry when one of us keels over or is shot by terrorists. Mum said she is willing to take her chances.

Thursday 22

Mum has rung Granny Clegg to see how the hip of doom is this morning and if it has foretold any more deaths in the night. Granny Clegg says it is much better but that she is still investigating yesterday's premonition (i.e. popping over to see Maureen in the Spar every half hour to check gossip on local illnesses and deaths).

Friday 23

It is James's birthday tomorrow. He says it is his coming of age. It is not. He will be ten, which is admittedly double figures, but is not sixteen, which is what I will be in less than five months' time. Hurrah! Have bought James a label maker from WHSmith. He is not having a proper party after last year's near-death experience at the Lord Butler Leisure Centre. He is having three friends to tea i.e. Mad

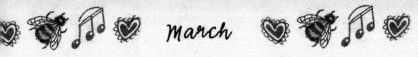
Harry, Maggot, and Keanu. Mum is not happy about Keanu but James insists. It is because he will get demoted gang-wise if Keanu is not permitted entry. Mum is going to hide all the valuables in her combination lock suitcase.

Saturday 24

James says it is his best birthday present haul yet. As well as the label maker, he got a book about frogs (Mum and Dad), a packet of frog mince (the dog), a talking Madonna doll (Grandpa and Treena), and a power drill (Granny and Grandpa Clegg—it cost £5.99 from Trago Mills. They had left the label on as usual.) Mum says he is only allowed to use the drill, and doll, under adult supervision. She means herself. Dad is not classed as an adult in her book.

5.30 p.m.
Got home from hard day at work to find Mum scraping misspelt labels off all the furniture and James banished to his bedroom. Apparently Keanu took control of the label machine and has labelled everything in the house, including the dog. But he cannot spell and so it says 'GOD' on its forehead. Which could not be further from the truth. Also the table says 'TAYBEL', the bathroom says 'TOYLIT', and Dad has one on his back that says 'MENTIL'.

Thank God I am going round Justin's tomorrow. He and Sad Ed are lucky to be only children. They have never

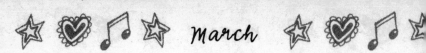
known what it is to suffer the horror of sibling rivalry. Or sibling idiocy.

Sunday 25

Summer Time begins (i.e. clocks go annoyingly forward)

Went round to Justin's at three as arranged but he was still in bed due to non-changing of clocks in Statham household. I am definitely going to write to the Prime Minister to complain. It is utterly inconvenient. Did some groupie work at band practice, i.e. snogged Justin heavily after triumphant guitar solo.

Also, it turns out Justin is not an only child. He has a twenty-one-year-old stepsister called Kelly who is a runner at GMTV. She gets to make tea and is in charge of emergency hairspray. It is the height of glamour. Am going to get to know her at first opportunity so she can get me a job one day. I am practically family so she cannot refuse me.

Monday 26

There is a suspicious pile of dog poo on our drive. It is definitely not the dog as he is over a mile away pooing happily on the Whiteshot Estate. Mum has cleared it up using industrial rubber gloves and James's Bob the Builder spade (now quarantined). She is thinking of reviving her

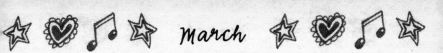

anti-dog-poo campaign in the *Walden Chronicle*. I hope not. It did not do my reputation at school any good amongst the dog-owning mafia. She says she has her suspicions anyway. They lie with Fiddy, Thin Kylie's annoying yapping thing, also former lover of dog, and mother to his equally mental offspring Bruce (now resident at Granny Clegg's).

5 p.m.

I hope it is dog poo and not possibly menacing man poo. He was back again after school today, reading *Elle Decoration*. Although maybe he is just admiring our double glazing and creosote fence.

Tuesday 27

There is more dog poo this morning. Mum took it straight over to Thin Kylie's on the smelly Bob spade. But Cherie is denying everything. She says it is too big to be one of Fiddy's, hers are more like chipolatas and our suspicious poo is like a saveloy. Which is true. Mum is going to ring the council later to demand an anti-dog-poo sign.

4 p.m.

The council say they cannot put up an anti-dog-poo sign as their pooing dog stencil is broken. She asked what other animals they had. They said cows or turkeys (there is a turkey farm on the Haverhill road and the turkeys are notoriously

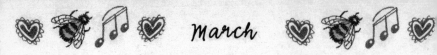

cunning at escaping and wandering aimlessly around the B1057). Mum hung up. She does not want a pooing farm animal picture up outside the house. She says it may confuse the perpetrator into thinking domestic dog poo is acceptable.

Wednesday 28

Poo on drive again. Although this time it was wrapped in a peach-scented nappy bag. Mum now thinks it might be the milkman. She says he has been waging a vendetta against us since her dairy-free stance. She has already accused him of overjangling his bottles at 6 a.m. She is going to intercept him tomorrow morning.

Thursday 29

Mum was up at five to intercept the milkman but was thwarted by total absence of poo. She tackled him anyway but he says he is more of a cat person. Then he tried to get her to sign up for yoghurts so she came back in before he could befuddle her with his marketing pitch. He has no chance, no one has ever befuddled her before, not even the Kleeneze man, and he once got Marjory to buy a gross of 'Christmas'-scented plug-in air fresheners. (He was also the recipient of one of James's pedant letters on the grounds that Christmas has no official smell.)

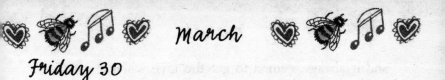

March

Friday 30

Last day of school. It is also the last day that Emily Reeve has to wear school uniform. It is because her bump cannot fit under the regulation kilt any more so Mr Wilmott has given her permission to wear concealing smocks etc. She has still not confessed to me who the father is. I have tried to reach out across the nylon carpet to offer my hand of friendship but she will not shake it. It is her loss. I would be an excellent confidante. I am utterly good at keeping secrets. I lasted three days when Scarlet told me she fancied the Incredible Hulk (green version, not Bruce thingy) before I told Sad Ed.

Also, the poo is back. Mum says it is the final straw. She is going to stay up all night to catch the culprit in the act. I said she would never manage it but she says she has stocked up on Nescafé and has the new Alan Titchmarsh novel to plough through.

Saturday 31

Oh my God. The dog is the phantom poo menace after all! Mum caught Grandpa letting him do it behind the Passat at midnight. She hauled him inside for interrogation (Grandpa, not the dog. The dog does not respond to questioning of any sort.) and he caved under pressure and admitted it was him all along. He said he was just taking the dog for a long walk

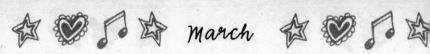

and it always seemed to get the urge when it got to our house. So Mum demanded to know why he was going on long walks late at night and Grandpa confessed it is to avoid Treena and her sexual demands. (That is what the ginseng was for after all!) He says he is too old to cope with her nightly pawings and he fears his heart might give way. Mum said what about Wednesday night (the mysterious no-poo night). He said *Dirty Dancing* was on ITV2 so Treena was glued to Patrick Swayze and he could rest in bed in peace. Mum is outraged. She has told him that the dog is to poo on its own doorstep from now on or she will be forced to take sanctions. (I wonder what these would be?) Then Grandpa got all teary and said he was seventy-five tomorrow and it was near the end for him and all he seemed to get was shouted at by women these days. So Mum felt sorry for him and made him a cup of Bovril and gave the dog a custard cream. But not that sorry because she refused to let him sleep on the sofa and sent him back to sex-crazed Treena at 2 a.m.

Bought something called Goat Weed off Mr Goldstein at work. Rosamund says it is an ancient libido-restoring herb. Am going to give it to Grandpa at his birthday party tomorrow, along with Suzy's phone number.

I'm RACHEL RILEY
— welcome to my so-called life.

April

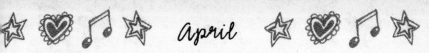

April

Sunday 1
Palm Sunday

8 a.m.

Am up and going to Scarlet's imminently. It is because Glastonbury tickets go on sale at 9 a.m. and we need to be poised with the interwebnet and Suzy's credit card (she has agreed to fund me and Sad Ed and we are going to pay her back on a twenty-five-year interest-free loan plan). Am utterly excited. Although getting a ticket is a minor hurdle compared to actually persuading Mum to let me go. Justin is going to do his at home. He does not need Suzy's funding. His dad owns a chain of bathroom shops.

11 a.m.

Oh my God! Have got a ticket for Glastonbury! Hurrah. Hurrah. Will get to wear patterned wellies and trilby hat whilst drinking hot cider and listening to seminal music. Scarlet says it is a total rite of passage and I am now in a very exclusive club. Along with 125,000 other chosen few. Which sadly does not include Sad Ed. He has been turned down! Suzy says it is not personal, it is a lottery. She is wrong. It is bound to be because he is not edgy-looking enough. Also, he applied under his real name of Edward Arthur Thomas, whilst I am Ray Riley! Scarlet and I are planning our wardrobe already. We are going to share a tent. She will be in one compartment with Trevor and me and Justin will be in the storage bit. She says their sex noises will

109

not keep us awake as they will be drowned out by repetitive drumming, druid chanting, and drug-induced vomiting on the tent pegs. It sounds excellent. But will not tell Mum yet. Need to formulate excellent plan and wear her down gently.

2 p.m.
Justin has not got a ticket for Glastonbury. He says he does not care as it is overcommercial and frequented only by wannabes, liggers, and Radio 1 DJs. Hurrah. It sounds excellent. Although it is sad that he is not coming, obviously.

4 p.m.
Grandpa and Treena came over with Jesus and the dog for celebratory diamond jubilee birthday party lunch. Grandpa Riley delighted with Suzy's phone number. Not so delighted with goat weed. He says there is no way he is consuming urine again. Asked him why he had drunk urine in first place. He said it was during World War Two when he was marooned in a Navy frigate off the coast of Africa. Mum reminded him yet again that he was only seven when World War Two started and that the Navy had turned him down for entry three times on height, eyesight, and intelligence grounds. So he said it must have been on holiday then. His memory is definitely going. Mum says it is just selective, like his hearing i.e. he pretends to be deaf when it suits him, which is often, i.e. whenever anyone tells him to do something he doesn't want to do, like stop eating all the Twiglets, or take the dog for a walk. But Grandpa says it is

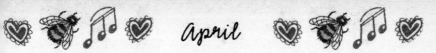
a sure sign he is on his way out. He is not. He is just fishing for compliments.

Monday 2

Hurrah, it is the holidays. Although they will sadly not be spent in usual manner i.e. watching *Friends* repeats on sofa with dog and James, as am now full-time employee of Nuts In May. Mr Goldstein phoned at eight this morning. Rosamund has decided to go on an emergency yogic retreat to restore her chakra and he cannot cope alone due to high shelves and hunchback. Anyway, it is excellent as will practically be able to pay Suzy back her Glastonbury money by the end of the week.

6 p.m.
Hurrah. Have been promoted to till in absence of Rosamund. It is excellent fun. Although actually quite tricky as till is vicious and has trapped fingers several times. Have acquired new-found admiration for Waitrose cashiers. Which is very left-wing and pro-working class. May even join union.

Tuesday 3

6 p.m.
Till down £13.73. Mr Goldstein has docked it out of my

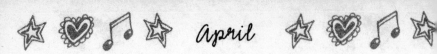
wages. Also have plasters on two fingers due to till injury. May ask to go back to stocking muesli.

Also, Dad has had a funny phone call at work. Someone called Mr Jones rang on pretext of querying a paperclip invoice and then just breathed heavily into receiver. This happened three times. Dad says he is probably just someone from Walton and Walton, as they are all 'hilarious' practical jokers. Mum says he should report them immediately as practical jokes are a menace and can easily get out of hand. This is after the time Grandpa Riley taught James to stretch clingfilm over the toilet seat and dog got entangled and stopped breathing for several seconds—it was trying to drink out of toilet bowl.

Wednesday 4

6 p.m.

Am sick of full-time work. Do not know how anyone copes with it. It is will-sapping, and finger-maiming stuff. Have bruises where hand actually got trapped in the pound coin drawer and Mr Goldstein had to free me with a stick of coltsfoot rock. No wonder Rosamund needs to restore her chakra. The only consolation is that Justin is on full-time mincing duty too so I get to watch his muscly arms ramming bits of cow into the grinder all day. It is a thing of beauty.

Also, Dad has had another four heavy breathing phone calls. He has taken tomorrow off in a bid to throw the perpetrator off-track.

Thursday 5

Asked Mr Goldstein where exactly in India Rosamund had gone to. He said she is not in India, she is in a barn in Steeple Bumpstead with a man called Guru Derek.

Also, telephone menace has tracked Dad down at Summerdale Road. There has been a funny phone call at home. James answered in his fake Dad voice (freakishly accurate) and then just got an earful of panting. I said it might be the dog as it has been known to knock phone off hook at Grandpa's and then lick it madly but James says the dog has never said, 'You're mine, Colin Riley. You're mine.'

Mum has called the police. She says terrorists are tracking Dad's every movement and are obviously ready to pounce and that they should have listened when she warned them about the *Grazia*-reading hooligan on Thin Kylie's wall. They are sending an officer round to interview Dad.

10 p.m.

Police say evidence suggests it is not terrorists, but just run-of-mill pervert, as they cannot trace any link between law-abiding non-Muslim Colin Riley and any potential Al Qaeda splinter cells operating in the area. Mum said she wasn't aware there were any Al Qaeda operatives in Saffron Walden. But PC Doone said we are all (he does not mean we, he means Muslims) guilty until proven innocent. I said wasn't it supposed to be the other way round, but he said I have been watching too much *Morse* and modern policing

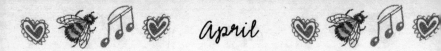

is all about suspecting everyone. I countered by saying he had been watching too much *Midsomer Murders* but he says he is more of a *Murphy's Law* man. Then Mum made him leave as the TV detective conversation was threatening to get out of hand and was not helping at all in the hunt for Dad's stalker. PC Doone said we should be looking closer to home because it is always the person you least expect. Dad is now watching Mum's every move. Mum is watching James. And James is watching the frogs.

Friday 6
Good Friday

Hurrah, no work. Mr Goldstein has shut up shop for the day due to everyone being too busy panic-buying hot-cross buns and giant Toblerones to stock up on sunflower seeds. House is a hotbed of who is stalking Dad controversy though. Even Clive next door is under suspicion. Mum made him breathe into the phone when he came round to borrow the long-handled secateurs. Dad and James have ruled him out though as his panting wasn't deep and throaty enough.

11 a.m.
Oh my God. The menacing man is back. James and I are watching him through the binoculars. He is reading *Tatler* at the moment. But he could flip any minute and firebomb us.

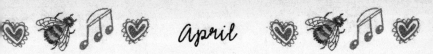

Mum has called the police again but they are permanently engaged. (It is due to Easter revving at Barry Island. The sugar and e-numbers send the O'Gradys into joy-riding frenzies.)

11.15 a.m.
Menacing man now fiddling with mobile phone. Maybe he is sending for reinforcements. Oh God. We are all doomed.

11.20 a.m.
Oooh. Our phone is ringing. Hope it is Justin. I will need to say goodbye if I am going to be murdered by fundamentalists any minute.

11.25 a.m.
Mum picked up. It was not Justin. Or three-minute bomb warning. It was heavy breathing phone menace. Mum says it is too much of a coincidence that menacing man is on phone at same time. She is going out. Have warned her that he may be suicide bomber with explosives strapped to his chest. But Mum says suicide bombers do not wear Marks & Spencer macs. Dad is watching from behind the curtain.

11.30 a.m.
It is worse than Mum (and Dad) feared! Menacing man and phone pervert is not Al Qaeda minion or even man, but is Edie Weeks, née Wilmott! She has been dressing up in Mr Wilmott's clothes and lurking about in hope of catching a glimpse of Sex Beast Riley. (Although why Mr Wilmott has

a balaclava is entirely suspicious. May report him to police as potential Al Qaeda operative. Would make excellent detective. Maybe they will ask me to join force and I will be youngest ever DCI!) Anyway, after Mum whipped the balaclava off, Scooby-Doo style, Edie confessed all, in her throaty, Rothman-ruined voice. She says she has never got over Dad and her life will be meaningless if she cannot have him. Mum said it is tough luck as he is very much not on the market any more. Then Edie broke down and wept all over the John Lewis rug and Mum had to call Mr Wilmott to take her away.

Dad did not come out from behind the curtain until Edie had been safely removed from the crime scene. It is not because he is scared of Edie, it is because he is scared of Mum. He has had a temporary reprieve anyway because Mum has taken James and has driven off in Fiesta. Oh God. Just had awful thought. What if she has walked out on us? She has taken her favourite child (i.e. James) with her and run away to Granny Clegg's and left me and Dad to fend for ourselves. He will have burned house to ground by Monday in chip pan fire and I will be in care and will never see Justin again. Oh God, the image of the Fiesta disappearing round Loompits Way is the last I will ever see of her. Must burn it onto brain so I do not forget her.

2 p.m.
Mum and James back. They had not run away to Cornwall but to Premier Travel to get brochures for emergency break.

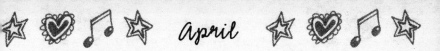

Mum says it is the only way to wean Edie off Dad. I said flying to the Bahamas would be an excellent place for us all to recover from the trauma and could I bring Justin but Mum says *a*) she has already ruled out all long-haul destinations due to James's persistent travel sickness issues and *b*) no I cannot. So then I begged to be left at home revising but she says I cannot be trusted to spend a week with my head in books and not mooning about over that 'long-haired layabout' (she does not consider 'rock musician' a valid career choice).

Ooh, I wonder where we will be going though. Maybe behind (now drawn back) iron curtain to visit war-ravaged villages. Or possibly to a souk in Morocco, where we will abandon our Western ways and frolic in kaftans and smoke hookah pipes.

Saturday 7

We are not going to souk. We are going to a French gîte in somewhere called St Abattage. Mum says it will be excellent for my GCSE revision and has lifted her embargo on continental travel especially. I have instructions to tell Mr Goldstein that I will not be available to sift lentils next Saturday. I also have instructions to say my goodbyes to Justin tonight as we are leaving for the ferry at five in the morning and I need to pack sensibly. Am not too depressed as it is utterly romantic and Jane Austenish to be kept apart by scheming parents. Also Johnny Depp has a house

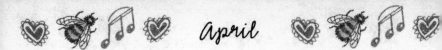

in France. He is utterly tragic and edgy and we would be excellent friends, despite the age gap. Oooh. Maybe he lives in St Abattage to keep away from glare of media. I can befriend him and we can discuss existential cinema in French whilst sipping Bordeaux and eating offensive cheese.

10 p.m.
Am home after very intense pre-separation snogging session during which I lost all control and let Justin put his hand inside jumper (but not inside Brownie T-shirt— am not total slut, yet). Have told him I will write to him every day but he said to call instead as the letters will take weeks if they get here at all. I said I only had £2.10 of minutes left but he has lent me his £50 Christmas present minutes voucher in case of emergency. I can pay him back from my Nuts In May wages. Once I have paid off doll and Suzy.

10.15 p.m.
Oops. Have not packed. Will just throw some things in a case in the morning. Hurrah. By ten tomorrow will be sipping café au lait with Johnny Depp in picturesque St Abattage.

Sunday 8
Easter Day

10 a.m.
Am not in picturesque St Abbatage but stuck in ferry

queue at Dover. There is a strike on the French side of the Channel. Dad says it is probably over the filling in their over-subsidized baguette lunches. Will call Scarlet to find out. She has inside information on all matters left wing. Mum is seething. She has entire holiday planned on a very strict itinerary and this is messing with all her food and toilet-stop timings. Have eaten entire Easter egg haul already (pitifully low this year due to Granny Clegg's hip of doom preventing her stalking the aisles of Trago Mills for cut price chocolate).

11 a.m.
Strike is not over baguette fillings. It is over the colour of their uniform. Also have had lengthy chat with Scarlet about possible new lyrics. She says 'Bad Bat Boy' is excellent but we need fresh material. Will start as soon as we settle into our inspiring French country retreat.

12 noon
Colour of uniform obviously agreed on as we are now on board ferry.

12.15 p.m.
Ferry departs British waters.

12.20 p.m.
Mum has panic attack due to sudden realization that frogs have been left home alone and may cause all manner

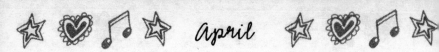

of hoo-ha when they make inevitable bid for freedom. (Note that she is not concerned that they may die of mince-starvation.) She instructs Steward Barry 'Hi, How Can I Help You' (freakishly small hands, severe dandruff, definitely gay) to inform captain of *Spirit of Adventure* of impending frog-related catastrophe and demand that he turn boat around immediately and return to English waters.

12.30 p.m.

Barry 'Hi, How Can I Help You' informs Mum it is not like *Miami Vice* and captain cannot just swing boat around in middle of Channel, and anyway it is not a boat it is a ferry. Mum commandeers Dad's phone to make emergency phone call to Marjory to get her to break in and confiscate frogs. James is staying strangely silent throughout. Maybe he is in shock due to possible demise of Ninja frogs.

12.45 p.m.

Marjory reports back that she cannot break through Mum's excessive security arrangements but that Clive went up a ladder to observe any signs of frog escape in James's bedroom and says lid is on but he cannot see frogs in tank at all. Mum says they may have gone already and covered up their tracks by replacing lid, and to call police if she hears any strange noises. James still silent.

12.50 p.m.
James says he is feeling possibly travel sick and goes to toilets.

1.15 p.m.
James still not back from seasickness episode. Mum says we are perilously close to French shores and she does not want him getting left on board like on the Safari Boat at Longleat. Dad despatched with box of wet wipes to investigate and possibly mop up.

1.20 p.m.
James discovered locked in disabled toilet. Not with head in loo but giving Donatello and Michaelangelo a swim in sink. He had smuggled them on board inside his Ninja Turtles lunchbox and they were getting dehydrated. Mum said we must hand them in to the authorities at once but Dad said we could get arrested for importing livestock into a restricted zone and the best plan is to conceal them in the Passat.

1.30 p.m. GMT (aka 2.30 CET i.e. French time)
Passat departs *Spirit of Adventure* with passengers safely strapped in seats and illegal immigrants (i.e. frogs) safely hidden in glove compartment with soggy wet wipes for survival. Mum gets stack of French maps out but Dad says we will not be needing them and sets trusty sat nav to continental mode. Sat nav estimates arrival time in St Abattage as 7.45

i.e. just in time for steak frites in local rustic bistro. Mum adjusts itinerary, cutting out three toilet stops and one meal. Entire car synchronizes watches, taking account of having 'time travelled' an hour ahead.

1.45 p.m.

Passat stops at Carrefour to purchase emergency mince as frogs are getting restless and croaking noisily inside their plastic prison.

5 p.m.

Sat nav estimates distance left as 130 miles.

5.30 p.m.

Sat nav estimates distance left as 150 miles. Mum demands a change from male voice to female as the man sat nav is obviously not so hot at map reading. Dad tries to explain the technical points of satellite navigation but Mum makes lips go thin and he switches to female mode.

5.45 p.m.

Female sat nav claims we are at our destination. Passat stops and Dad investigates. We are in middle of motorway. Sat nav returned to more authoritative male mode.

6 p.m.

Sat nav man claims we are in Latvia. Dad hits sat nav. Sat nav man goes ominously silent. Mum retrieves stack of

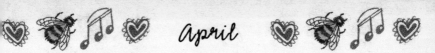
French maps from boot of car. We are not in Latvia. We have detoured to somewhere called Marly le Roi, i.e. several hundred miles from St Abattage. Mum reestimates arrival time at 10 p.m. precisely.

6.15 p.m.
James banned from saying, 'Are we nearly there yet?' (In fact a reinforcement of an earlier ban, as it was initially imposed five years ago after particularly traumatic Easter queues on the A303 to Cornwall.)

8 p.m.
Passat stops for dinner on verge. Not steak frites but in fact Marmite sandwiches and satsumas. Or mince, in case of frogs.

8.10 p.m.
Mum packs everyone back into car in accordance with her rigid itinerary.

10 p.m.
Passat arrives at gîte. Mum claims victory over sat nav, and Dad, as he is responsible for transport (she is responsible for accommodation and activities).

10.10 p.m.
Dad claims victory over Mum as electricity in gîte not working.

10.15 p.m.

Mum claims victory over Dad as torch is missing from car emergency toolkit.

10.20 p.m.

James claims victory over everyone as he has packed his Tweenies torch (in lunchbox with frogs, in case they got scared of dark).

10.30 p.m.

Riley family clean teeth by torchlight and retire to rooms. Frogs retire to temporary shelter arrangement in what is presumed to be kitchen, though is hard to tell in dark. Am too tired to unpack. Will do it in morning. Will just phone Justin quickly though to say goodnight.

11.30 p.m.

Just put phone down. It is excellent that there is clear phone reception in the middle of nowhere. The French are obviously uber-efficient at communication matters. Unlike the Cornish who have patchy coverage at best, and none at all in Granny Clegg's house. It is a shame Justin is stuck in Saffron Walden though and not here in France enjoying ancient stone gîte in rural idyll, where the only sound is the murmur of wildlife.

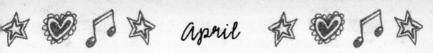
Monday 9

Easter Monday (Bank Holiday UK and Rep. Ire.)

5 a.m.
Wildlife murmur escalated to shrieking sound. It is inconsiderate French chicken heralding dawn outside room.

5.15 a.m.
Chicken is not outside room but is busy heralding inside room. It must have sneaked in when we arrived. Or maybe it lives here. Mum has given it a hefty thwack with her sheepskin slipper and it has disappeared downstairs somewhere. Although now it has set frogs into croaking frenzy. Wish was back in Saffron Walden listening to drone of minibikes and distant M11 traffic. Am going back to sleep.

8 a.m.
Hurrah. Have had excellent extra beauty sleep and am now up and ready to investigate historic St Abattage. Will get dressed after breakfast of croissants and hot chocolate.

9 a.m.
No croissants. Nearest baker is ten miles away and Dad is refusing to drive due to his hands being welded in steering wheel position following yesterday's epic journey. And Mum is refusing to take us as she can only drive Fiestas and only on the right side of the road, i.e. the left. Also no hot

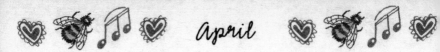

chocolate due to continuing electricity issue (gîte still in semi-darkness). Ate Marmite on stale Waitrose wholemeal and drank warm Evian. Frogs ate mince. Dad now in damp-smelling cellar looking for fusebox with Tweenies torch. Also, why did I not pack properly? Have managed to bring bridesmaid's dress with me. Why did I think that would be useful? It is not even wearable at a wedding any more due to compost stains. Also, did not pack books so am destitute, literature-wise. Mum says she will lend me a Maeve Binchy or Rosamund Pilcher. I said no thanks as will perish intellectually. She said well it's that or James's *Young Bond*. Have borrowed the Maeve Binchy. Will start reading once have explored history-steeped medieval St Abattage.

10 a.m.
Have investigated St Abattage with James. It is not history-steeped medieval village at all but French equivalent of Cornish backwater St Slaughter, complete with straw-chewing inmates. There are no magic Chocolat shops, à la Juliette Binoche, and absolutely no Johnny Depp. There is a café full of old men smoking Gitanes, a car mechanic called Monsieur Voiture, and a French Spar run by a woman with one eyebrow. Thank God I have contact with outside world. Am going to phone Justin immediately.

11 a.m.
Am off phone. Dad has discovered electricity. Not in

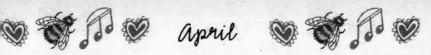

Thomas Edison way but has located fusebox behind pile of damp mattresses. Lights are on and revealing catalogue of substandard accommodation issues as follows:

1. Gîte is not *Elle Decoration*-style rural retreat but breeze-block stable conversion in Granny Clegg Decoration style, i.e. swirly carpet, pictures of dogs in hats playing snooker, and excess Formica.

2. Shelves do not contain vast collection of GCSE-improving French literature, as imagined by me. In fact contain china shepherdess display and brass clock (not working).

3. Bathroom is infested by grotesque insect life. Is like episode of David Attenborough every time you need the loo, causing several wee-on-wall accidents in case of James. Frogs have been installed in sink to prey on them. But this means cleaning teeth in bath as frogs do not like minty spit.

4. There is a chicken living in the cellar (it has access via a gigantic hole in the wall). Dad discovered it when it pecked him on the head during the hunt for electricity. He is going to block the hole later once the chicken has gone out.

5. Electricity supply is entirely random i.e. lights go on and off for no apparent reason. James is enjoying it and says it is like being at a disco but Mum is concerned strobe effect may cause fits.

These have been catalogued and are now running against Mum in unofficial 'who organizes best holiday?' competition.

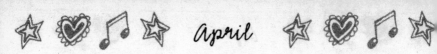
Mum is countering by organizing lunch trip to authentic village café. She will not be beaten. Hurrah. Will be sipping Pinot Noir shortly in continental manner (it is compulsory for children to drink wine in France).

5 p.m.

Lunch at authentic village café (the ambitiously-named Café de Paradis) was suspicious soup consumed in fog of Gitanes fumes. Also did not get to drink wine. Got warm Evian. Mum says she learnt her lesson after Thin Kylie's birthday party when I did purple Pernod sick several times. Dad says it is another point to him but Mum has trumped him with the revelation that the village has a bistro and we are booked in for a steak frites supper (or *le croque monsieur* in her case as she does not trust French to have eliminated mad cow disease). Hurrah. I expect it will be actually Michelin-starred restaurant that people drive hundreds of miles to just to sample their peasant cuisine.

8 p.m.

Was not Michelin-starred restaurant. Was not even bistro. Was Café de Paradis but with candles stuck in old Ricard bottles and extra Gitanes fog. Ate more suspicious soup under gaze of hostile locals. Mum and Dad are going to Carrefour tomorrow to stock up on tinned goods. Am now retiring to bed early due to utter lack of entertainment/literary stimulation/electricity. But not before have just had quick chat with Justin.

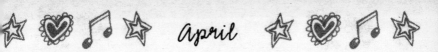

10.30 p.m.

Phone has gone dead. Think may have used up all minutes. Will just borrow Dad's in future. He will not mind. It is all paid for by Wainwright and Hogg anyway.

Tuesday 10

10 a.m.

Woken at five again by chicken in cellar. It has obviously fought its way back in through Dad's inadequate defences. (Point to Mum.) Plus chicken is a bad influence on the frogs. They are chorusing constantly now. James says it is a sure sign they are building up for their death match with Shredder. Reminded James that Shredder is a cartoon. He said, 'That's what they want you to think.' He has gone to Carrefour with Mum and Dad. He wants to be sure they purchase essential items like Shreddies. Am going on mind-expanding trip to museum when they get back. Hope it is better than Cornish Museum of Mines. That is just a dark passageway and some ancient pasty remnants.

5 p.m.

Museum not better than Museum of Mines. It was Museum of Footwear (seriously). Exhibition consisted of Neanderthal socks, a piece of leather allegedly from one of Napoleon's war boots, and some trainers (not even Nikes), to represent

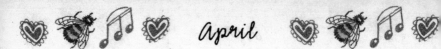

Modern Man. It was all *complètement ordure* (note excellent use of French). Only James seemed happy. It is because they had an 'interactive display' where you could measure your own feet. I said he could do that at Debarrs for nothing but he said it is not the same as the numbers there are not in French. He is a *grand imbècile*.

8 p.m.

Have eaten tea (Bird's Eye fishfingers and peas). Lights currently out so cannot possibly do any revision. On plus side, darkness makes it easy to borrow Dad's phone. Will just call Justin to say goodnight and obtain Saffron Walden gossip.

10 p.m.

Nothing is happening in Saffron Walden as usual. Unless you count Mr Patel's controversial new neon shop sign. Asked Justin what he was doing to while away hours until I return. He says he is playing his guitar and wandering aimlessy around the Waitrose snack aisle. He is definitely in love, no matter what Scarlet says.

Wednesday 11

5 a.m.

How does chicken know what time it is? It is accurate to the second.

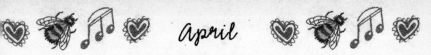
10 a.m.

Mum has pointed out that have been here three days and I have not communicated properly with any locals i.e. am going to fail my GCSE. I pointed out that I had asked one-eyebrowed woman in Spar for '*le chocolat, s'il vous plaît*' earlier. But Mum says that is not A* grade material. She says I am in charge of all communication with foreigners today. This does not bode well. We are going to Café de Paradis again for lunch later. Mum says it will be fine if we sit outside to avoid fumes.

2 p.m.

Lunch not entirely successful due to less than A* conversational French from Rachel Riley. Think have possibly eaten horse. Also Dad got apple pie in gravy due to slight confusion between pommes and pommes de terre. We are off to vineyard now. At least will not have to talk too much there. Will just nod at interesting grapes. Have asked Mum if can at least gargle and spit wine out in authentic manner. She says as long as she can see visible spitting.

5 p.m.

James has been sick down side of Passat. Mum was so busy checking that I was spitting she forgot to monitor James. He had swallowed several glasses of vin rouge before Dad noticed he was behaving erratically (i.e. not asking a million questions and taking notes). (Mum is claiming victory as she says sick incident occurred during transport phase of visit.) I on other hand spat in professional manner and also used

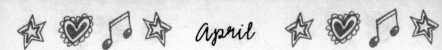
several excellent French words like '*superbe*', '*magnifique*', and '*zut alors*'. Am totally going to get A*.

8 p.m.
James asleep in darkened room with bucket and Cillit Bang (brought from home in case of just such an emergency) next to bed in readiness.

Thursday 12

5.05 a.m.
Chicken gone off boil. It is five minutes late this morning. But making up for inaccuracy by issuing single, earshattering scream. Am going to reinforce damp mattress defences later when have recovered from shock.

10 a.m.
James is still actually green. He says he has learnt his lesson and will be staying away from the demon drink for the rest of his life. He has declined a visit to Europe's largest sausage factory and has taken to his sick bed again with a glass of Evian and a dry cracker. Have also declined invitation on grounds that I can watch Justin do it for free every Saturday. Instead have purchased *Le Monde* from monobrow Spar woman and am going to immerse myself in current affairs, French-style. Chicken is safely locked out (hole reinforced with fertilizer sack) and Dad has left

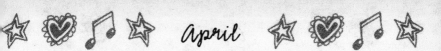
phone in case of emergency. I am to call *les police* in cases of the following: fire, flood, possible perverts, or attack from hostile forces.

10.15 a.m.
Le Monde is not as easy as I thought. Have just read article that seems to imply Nicolas Sarkozy eats cats. Or maybe it is true. The French are renowned for embracing exotic foodstuffs.

10.30 a.m.
Oops. Just remembered am supposed to be doing band practice with Scarlet tonight. Will just call her quickly to remind her am in France. It is emergency after all.

11 a.m.
Ooh. And Sad Ed to find out how Edie is dealing with utter rejection by Sex Beast Riley.

11.01 a.m.
Must stop calling him that. He is not Sex Beast. He is Dad.

12.15 p.m.
Edie is back in rehab. Apparently Mr Wilmott found her slumped across the polished pine kitchen table with the entire contents of his drinks cabinet inside her (half a bottle of brandy and a litre of Advocaat). It is so unfair. Mum would never do that. I may well raise a formal complaint

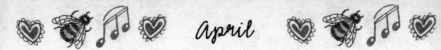
as it is completely holding me back, literary-wise, having such normal parents. Their normality could be the reason for me failing English GCSE. Ooops. And French GCSE. Had better return to *Le Monde*.

12.30 p.m.
Am bit peckish. Will just eat stimulating French lunch (aka Marmite sandwich).

1.30 p.m.
Ooh—just remembered, Scarlet said we need new material for Battle of Bands. Will write about inspiring experiences in France. That is almost as good as conjugating verbs. Will be like Jim Morrison writing 'Spanish Caravan'. Will call it 'French Gîte'. Possibly.

2 p.m.
Breeze-block gîte not entirely inspiring source for song. Also, chicken is watching me through window menacingly. May go for inspiring walk in village.

4 p.m.
Oh God. Something terrible has happened. The chicken has killed Donatello and Michaelangelo and eaten the evidence! (Frogs are missing and chicken is parading around bathroom with menacing look and bloodstained feathers.) It is also now refusing me entry to the bathroom. James will be devastated. Oh God. Where is James?

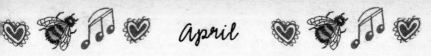

april

4.15 p.m.

James missing. Am calling police immediately. Think chicken may have killed and eaten him too. Is not chicken at all but one of those evil bird creatures out of *Harry Potter*. Have barricaded it in bathroom in case it comes after me next.

4.20 p.m.

Have rung police and informed them of emergency i.e. *Le poulet diabolique avez mangez mon frère et deux grenouilles.* Think they are coming soon.

4.30 p.m.

Oh, hope police hurry up. Chicken is throwing itself at door. It is like horror movie. A claw will get through the polished pine any second and then its beady eye will appear with my terrified face reflected in it. (Ooh, would make excellent horror writer. Maybe could be like female Stephen King and make millions from gruesome bestsellers but be snubbed by Booker judges for being populist. That is, if I survive the chicken attack.)

5 p.m.

Thank God. Can hear voices outside. Will throw myself at their mercy and let them take out the chicken with heavy artillery.

6 p.m.

Was not police. Was Mum and Dad with James. Chicken had not eaten him after all. Instead he had woken up and,

135

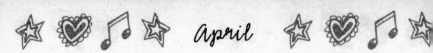
to his delight, found house empty and gone to village to buy lightbulbs, string, and paint. He was hoping to fulfil his lifelong ambition i.e. being left Home Alone, and battling burglars with ingenious gadgets. Told them not to enter house due to scene of utter carnage. Then it was like a slow motion bit in a film because James cried out, 'Donatello, Michaelangelo,' and dropped the lightbulbs and paint in his rush to save his Ninja frogs. Chicken seized its chance to escape and flew over his head and out of front door, taking remains of frogs with him. James is now being revived from shock with French chocolate milk (suspiciously named Cacolac). And I, on other hand, am shut in room without even Maeve Binchy for comfort as punishment for woeful inability to babysit. On plus side still have Dad's phone in pocket. Will just call Justin and tell him about my near-death experience.

8 p.m.
Justin says I am lucky to be alive and that he could not go on if I had been eaten by a giant chicken. (Exaggerated exact size of chicken a bit for effect.) I asked if he would have committed suicide à la Romeo. He said no, he meant he would not bother washing his hair for a week. Which is almost the same and totally romantic. Ooh. May write song about it all.

9 p.m.
Mum has just been in. The police have agreed to let me

off the false emergency phone call. Mum made them do it as she said she would report them for failing to respond to an emergency, false or otherwise, in sufficient time. ('Conversational French for the Over-40s' is obviously more useful than I imagined.) Also they have given her permission to use any force necessary to despatch the chicken. Have apologized for demise of frogs. She said I am forgiven. Think she is secretly relieved as she will not have to smuggle them back across the border now.

9.15 p.m.

James has just been in. He is revived by Cacolac and has a new mission. He thinks the chicken might actually be a Ninja now, because it has absorbed the powers of the frogs. He is going to catch it and tame it and bring it back to Saffron Walden to fight Shredder.

9.30 p.m.

Have written song. It is called 'Death Chicken'.

Death Chicken
Your eyes are full of menace
My heart is full of dread
You stalk me in my dreams at night
And peck me in the head
Death chicken (bloodcurdling squawk sound)
Death chicken

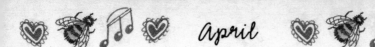

That is it. There was an excellent second verse about that film *The Birds* but could not think of anything to rhyme with Tippi Hedren.

Will just phone Scarlet and read her the lyrics.

11 p.m.
Scarlet says new song is very goth horror and could well secure our victory in Battle of Bands. She says she loves that it is allegorical about American politics. I agreed. Though have no idea what she means. Maybe I am so good it just happened subliminally. Also she says she has utterly incredible news. But that it is too huge to relate details over phone. It is bound to be about her and Trevor. Maybe they have broken up after all.

Am very tired after traumatic day. Thank God chicken has fled. Will be able to lie in in peace.

Friday 13

5 a.m.
Chicken is back (Friday the 13th style) and is louder than ever. As is Mum. She shouted, 'Colin, do something useful for once in your life.' Followed by Dad's unmistakable grumbling and heavy plod downstairs.

5.10 a.m.
Chicken silent. Dad has obviously chased it away. Thank God.

Although James will be disappointed at the disappearance of the new Ninja chicken.

9 a.m.
It is last day today so am going to Spar to purchase presents for Scarlet, Sad Ed, and Justin. Mum says I must be back by twelve as she is cooking celebratory French lunch.

12 noon
Present shopping not entirely successful due to woeful lack of tourist fayre in French Spar. Have got Cacolac for Sad Ed, Gitanes lighter for Scarlet (for incense sticks), and a Johnny Hallyday (no idea) bag for Justin. Will say it is ironic.

3 p.m.
Lunch was delicious and traditional French coq au vin. So got to drink wine. Sort of. Am glad am not still in vegetarian stance. The French are very unaccommodating when it comes to non-meat eaters, i.e. it is practically illegal.

5 p.m.
Have just had thought. Do not remember Mum bringing chicken back from Carrefour. And one-eyebrowed woman definitely does not stock poultry. Oh God. Think we may have eaten the death chicken. Which means we have also eaten Ninja frogs. Gross. Am going to confront Mum immediately.

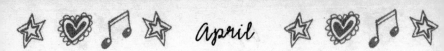

5.30 p.m.
It is true. Mum has confessed everything. She is unrepentant and says chicken is chicken and the frogs just add to the flavour. She will be sorry when I have told James of our cannibalism. He will be devastated.

6 p.m.
James not devastated. In fact is delighted as he now thinks not only has he avenged the deaths of the frogs, but he will have absorbed their powers. He is now checking himself for visible signs of Ninjahood. Also, apparently Dad killing menacing chicken with bare hands has inflamed Mum's passion as they have gone on romantic walk. Will exploit peace by calling Justin to remind him to meet me at the unhygienic phone box at nine tomorrow night (in accordance with return itinerary, sat nav issues pending).

Saturday 14

11 a.m.
Ooops. Have just woken up. As has everyone else in house. We are now two hours late according to our return itinerary. Mum is blaming Dad for killing the trusty, if annoying, chicken alarm clock. But Dad says he is used to relying on her waterworks waking him up when she goes for a wee and is blaming her uncharacteristically capacious bladder. Mum has responded by axing two wee stops and all food stops

from the return journey. We will have to eat sandwiches on the move. A reckless act, in my opinion, as crumbs in the car are one of Mum's banned items.

2 p.m.
Mum is making everyone hang out of window to eat sandwiches, risking near death from overtaking traffic, in James's case. Dad is being handfed by Mum with a Tupperware lid held under his chin to prevent spillage. According to Mum's maps we are 208 miles away from Calais and ferry is due to leave in three hours. James says we have no chance of making it unless Mum lifts her ban on exceeding sixty miles an hour. He says seventy mph is the bare minimum required. Mum has compromised on sixty-five.

4 p.m.
There are still eighty-two miles to go and only sixty minutes to do it in. But Mum is asleep so Dad is taking the daring move of driving at ninety miles an hour. He is very excited and thinks he is Jeremy Clarkson. He will not be so fuelled with testosterone when we hit the back of a Renault Megane and Mum bans him from driving ever again. Or, worse, makes him drive the Fiesta.

4.55 p.m.
Mum has just woken up but Passat is already safely on board the *Spirit of Adventure* and is, amazingly, dent and speeding ticket-free. She is thinking of writing to the RAC

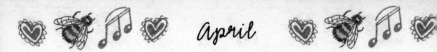

april

to inform them their map distances are all out. James (also asleep for most of journey) told her it is not distance but is because his Ninja powers allowed us to subvert the space-time continuum.

6 p.m.
Ferry still very much in French waters due to leaky hold. Barry (still gay with freakishly small hands and severe dandruff but now with ill-advised ash blond dye job) is handing out complimentary mints and sick bags while someone plugs hole. Oh God, am going to miss Justin at our pre-arranged snog. Ooh. Or maybe ferry will hit an iceberg in stormy ocean and will be like *Titanic* with me as Kate Winslet and we will fight with the people on Deck B (scabby deck) for spaces in the lifeboats. Hurrah.

8.45 p.m. CET (aka 7.45 p.m. GMT i.e. Saffron Walden time)
Ferry has docked in Dover with no *Titanic*-style incident. Have told Dad he has just over an hour to drive the 120 miles to Saffron Walden (i.e. ninety-six mph according to Ninja Riley). He says he does not know what I am thinking of, as he would never break the speed limit. James says he will use his Ninja powers again.

9 p.m.
Ninja powers not in evidence. Justin is waiting for me in a stinky phonebox outside the library whilst we are very

much on the M25. Have begged Dad to lend me his mobile but he says it is for emergencies only and my love life does not in any way constitute one, according to Wainwright and Hogg rules. Will not mention other 'emergencies' in France. He will never know. Bill probably gets paid by direct debit anyway.

10.30 p.m.

Am home. Will just call Justin to apologize for missed rendezvous (see, am still speaking French, it is like second nature now and am totally fluent). Will only be five minutes as Mum has strict rule on phone usage. Will not tell her I am calling his mobile. That is utterly banned.

11.30 p.m.

Hurrah. Justin is not at all cross that I did not turn up at the phonebox. He says Darryl Stamp set fire to the rubbish bins and it was 'mad'. Said I thought he would be above minor pyrotechnics what with him being artistic type etc., but he said there is nothing more interesting than watching chavs burn stuff. Maybe he is just in touch with his working-class roots (Mrs Statham is from Leytonstone, which is very *EastEnders*). That must be it. He is like Paul McCartney. Except without the jowls and maroon hair. Ooh. Wonder if I have time to find out Scarlet's amazing news? Will just call. Maybe she and Trevor have not broken up but have done 'It'!

12.15 a.m.

It is sex news. But not about Scarlet. It is about Jack. He is going out with Sophie Microwave Muffins! They got off with each other round at Melanie Shave's 'get the troops out' ironic tarts and vicars party. She says Justin doesn't know yet. I said why would he care? She said, 'Don't get minty with me, why do you care?' I said I am far from minty, I am just pointing out a fact. She said France has obviously made me continental and sulky and she will call me tomorrow when I am back to being English. She is right. I am tired from all the deep and meaningful French discussions. That and the killer chicken. That is why I am cross. Will sleep it off and be refreshed in morning and happy for Jack and his new love.

Sunday 15

Am not refreshed at all but have woken up in state of utter gloom. It is because of Jack and Sophie Microwave Muffins. They are utterly wrong for each other. It is like Jeremy Paxman going out with someone from the BBC canteen. Unlike me and Justin, which is love across a divide, which is totally different.

3 p.m.
Justin knows about Jack and Sophie Microwave Muffins. Scarlet just rang to tell me that Jack says Justin saw

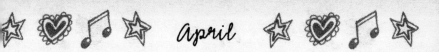
them walk past his house holding hands and gave them a definite dirty look. I said he must be mistaken as Justin does not get up until at least half three, but she says E4's schedule overhaul is causing havoc with Sixth Form lie-ins and that wake-up call is now midday. I said the dirty look was probably just tiredness then. She said, 'Get real.'

I am real. Unlike Sophie Microwave Muffins who is several shades lighter than Barry 'Hi, How Can I Help You' on the L'Oréal scale. Anyway. I do not care about Jack. I will be reunited with the ONE, i.e. Justin, in two hours and will do excellent snogging and may even let him touch my décolletage, now that I have been to France, which is renowned for being sexually liberated.

8 p.m.

Justin is in funny mood. He did not even do any French kissing let alone try to grope my décolletage. I said is this about Jack and Sophie Microwave Muffins and he said only because she and Jack are totally wrong for each other. Which at first I thought was a bad sign but on reflection it is actually good, because it is exactly what I thought. So we even think alike, we are so totally suited to each other, which proves even more that he is the ONE. In fact, am so inspired am going to write a song about it.

10 p.m.

Have written song. It is called 'Is She Really Going Out With

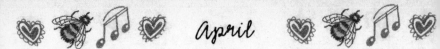
Him?' and is sort of to the tune of 'Sk8ter Boy'. (Which have also stolen some themes from. Only is not stealing, according to Scarlet, is postmodernism.)

> **Is She Really Going Out With Him?**
> *He watches news, BBC2,*
> *Documentaries on Africa,*
> *He plays the drums, writes his own songs,*
> *Based on books by Salinger.*
>
> *She reads* Heat, *thinks kittens are sweet,*
> *Thinks* Newsnight's *for geeks and flakes,*
> *Hates politics, says MPs make her sick,*
> *Thinks all parties come with cakes.*

Am still working on a chorus but think it has definite potential.

Monday 16

School is awash with Jack and Sophie Microwave Muffins excitement. Even Mrs Leech is banging on about it. She says it is like when political brain JFK married society beauty Jackie Onassis. I said it was more like his illicit liaison with glamorous but stupid Marilyn Monroe but Mrs Leech was too busy restocking her medical kit (i.e. emptying gypsy creams into a tin) to hear me.

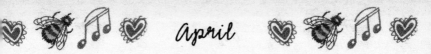

april

The Maths Club have already opened a book on them being named head boy and head girl in June. It is pathetic. They have only been going out for five minutes, unlike me and Justin who are celebrating three and a half months of snogging. Although there appears to be a current lull in proceedings. He turned down my offer to snog on the sheep field at first break in favour of lurking at the fruit and nut machine. Scarlet says he is hoping to overhear Jack and Sophie gossip but she is wrong. He is just upping his nut consumption for health reasons, he told me. And I have seen the KP packets to prove it.

Also, Sad Ed is depressed. (I mean, really depressed, as opposed to his usual state of perpetual gloom.) It is because Edie is threatening to move back to America to get over her rejection by Dad, which means Tuesday will have to go with her, which means he will be utterly single again and will have to work on his upper arm flab. We have called an emergency meeting at Scarlet's on Friday night. Suzy is going to chair.

Tuesday 17

Justin is revived by all the nuts. He says there is only one way to counter the Jack and Sophie Microwave Muffins phenomenon that is threatening our position as official edgiest and hottest couple, and that is to be even edgier and hotter.

12 noon

Plans to regain status as school couple *de jour* slightly thwarted. Justin threw me recklessy against the fruit and nut machine at lunchtime but the force made the machine dispense raisins all over the parquet and Mr Wilmott had to call the caretaker Lou to clean up. Justin said it was our chemistry but Lou said it was because my 'arse had jammed a knob the wrong way'. It would have been better if we had just lounged provocatively on the saggy sofa in the Sixth Form common room like Jack and Sophie Microwave Muffins. Except that not only has she got bigger breasts she is also sixteen i.e. legally allowed in the common room. Unlike me, who is only permitted to lounge on the sheep field which is damp and poo-ridden, as well as being infested by snogging Retards and Criminals.

Wednesday 18

Showed Scarlet lyrics for 'Is She Really Going Out With Him?' at band practice. Scarlet said, 'Is it about Jack and Sophie?' I said no it is totally made up about fictional characters. Like 'Bad Bat Boy and the Skinny Jeans'. She said that is about Trevor. I said *au contraire*, it is about universal issues of love and fashion. She did not look convinced but has agreed to include it in our set. She has no choice. The

competition is less than a fortnight away and we only have two songs. ('Death Chicken' has been axed on the grounds that it might incite violence against animals, only has one verse, and Scarlet cannot change from G to A minor that quickly.)

Cannot tell her song is about Jack. She will not understand our complicated relationship.

5 p.m.
I do not understand our complicated relationship.

6 p.m.
Not that we have a relationship.

Thursday 19

Granny Clegg's Easter eggs have finally arrived. They are squished irreparably. Mum told Granny Clegg she will complain to Royal Mail but Granny Clegg says they were like that when she bought them off Maureen for 50p. James says he does not mind eating broken chocolate pieces but Mum says the mess from the shards will be incalculable and she will melt them down for alternative use. If it is anything like when she melted down slivers of old soap to make new giant soap during an economy drive, the results are to be avoided at all costs.

Friday 20

Went round Scarlet's for emergency Edie summit. Justin was annoyed as it meant we could not snog in the bus shelter but I said this was a matter of life or death (not quite true but Sad Ed is threatening to stop speaking to me unless I find a way to keep Tuesday in the country—he is blaming me for Dad's unwillingness to cheat on Mum with Edie). I invited Justin to help us formulate a plan but he said he had better things to do than hang around with a twat. (He means Jack, who, I pointed out, was more likely to be in the bus shelter snogging Sophie Microwave Muffins but this seemed to make him more sulky.)

Anyway, Suzy had come up with a genius plan. It is to find someone else in Saffron Walden to go out with Edie so that she forgets about Dad completely. Suzy has compiled a list of potential suitors using her in-depth knowledge of all things sexual and relationshippy. There are three so far:

- PC Doone (Suzy says he has the potential to keep her on the straight and narrow and also she has it on good authority that he has a big willy);
- Mr Vaughan (no evidence of big willy, but definite supersize nipples);
- Barry the Blade (single, has also been in mental institution so they have something in common, and possibly desperate).

She also had Mr Wilmott on there, on the grounds he is perpetually single and in dire need of womanly comfort, until Sad Ed reminded her he was Edie's brother. Suzy has relisted him under possibles. She does not let taboo, or the law, stand in the way of love. She is going to matchmake by inviting them round to dinner. They will come for sure. She is a TV sex guru and Saffron Walden's biggest celebrity. (Marlon has moved back to Emmerdale and the least-famous McGann has been downgraded to not-at-all famous as people now think he just looks a bit like one of them and may be a lookylikey masquerader after all.)

Jack was not at the bus shelter. He was in his room. Could hear the unmistakable idiotic high-pitched laugh of Sophie Microwave Muffins piercing the kitchen ceiling every few minutes.

Saturday 21

There is no escape from Jack and Ms Muffins. I could clearly see them through the raisin display lurking in Goddard's this morning while Sophie bought a steak slice. It is obvious she does not appreciate Jack's vegetarian tendencies. If I was going out with him I would only bring him to Nuts In May, which is completely meat free (James checked, in case he could write one of his pedant letters).

Also Rosamund is back at work. Apparently Guru Derek has performed miracles and not just with her chakra, but

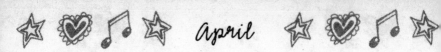

also on her eczema, tinnitus, tennis elbow, and persistent headlice. She says she has been reborn and has instructed us to call her Moonchild from now on. She is trying to persuade Mr Goldstein to let Derek touch his hunchback with his healing hands. Mr Goldstein says no one touches his hunch, not even Mrs Goldstein. So she asked if I had need of any miracles. I said yes but unless Guru Derek could shrivel 34C breasts then not to bother him. She said mine looked more like As than Cs to her so I sighed and went to restack the prunes.

Sunday 22

6 p.m.
Grandpa and the dog are back. They have been thrown out by Treena over their mismatched libidos (Grandpa's, not the dog's). Apparently the last straw came when Grandpa said he would rather watch *Look East* than massage Treena's buttocks with cooking oil. I do not blame him. It is punishment, not pleasure, to go near Treena's buttocks, especially with a bottle of Mazola.

Mum said at least he has not got custody of Jesus, but Grandpa says, *au contraire*, Treena is being very generous and has given him full visiting rights. Jesus will be coming to stay every weekend as well as several nights a week, i.e. whenever Treena goes to the Queen Elizabeth. Mum pointed out that, as Jesus is in nursery every day, this

means Treena does not actually do much looking after Jesus at all. But Grandpa says it is hard being a single mum and he is determined to do his bit during this trial separation. Mum said it had better be a trial one not an actual one.

Only James is delighted. He has a Ninja companion once again, i.e. the dog. He is going to train it to sniff out criminals and attack them with silent but deadly moves. He has no chance. The dog is a constant source of noise pollution. Also, it has no ability to spot criminals. It is always trying to lick Fat Kylie. It is the Snickers residue.

8 p.m.
Oooh. Have just had an excellent thought. Maybe Grandpa could go out with Edie. He is a Riley, after all, which could satisfy her obsession. And I would get wardrobe access without going into care. Plus I bet she is not as sexually demanding as Treena. All that vodka will have killed off her nerve endings.

Monday 23
St George's Day (England)

Grandpa Clegg rang to moan about St George's Day. It is not because he thinks it has been overtaken by flag-waving jingoists and possible racists like the Britchers (this is a good thing in his eyes), it is because he wants the government to

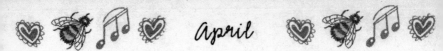

officially recognize St Piran's Day (i.e. the moronic patron saint of tin-miners, who sailed to Cornwall on a stone). He says he is thinking of signing up to fight the campaign for Cornish independence and that he is prepared to spill blood for his beliefs. Mum then pointed out that it is not an actual battle with swords like at the Civil War re-enactment at Bodmin four years ago. At which news Grandpa was apparently disappointed. Mum says she is not worried anyway. He is notoriously fickle when it comes to political campaigning, like the time he went shopping for pants instead of requesting an audience with the Prime Minister.

Tuesday 24

Have told Scarlet to tell Suzy to add Grandpa to Edie's list of single men. She says the first hot date is already scheduled for Thursday next week (vegetarian moussaka with PC Doone), but she will see if he can be squeezed in later in the month.

Also, Mum and Dad have been given the cholesterol all-clear by Bupa. I said it was a relief that the soya milk regime is finally over. But Mum said on the contrary, it is very much in place in order to maintain their clog-free arteries. Dad is having none of it though. I saw him eat eleven chocolate digestives while Mum popped over to Marjory's to borrow an Oxo cube.

Wednesday 25

The BBC (who never lie, in Mum's book) have reported that soya milk may cause cancer and sex change issues due to high oestrogen content. We are back on non-transgender semi-skimmed and Lurpak. The milkman is jubilant. He has signed Mum up for seven semi-skimmed, a six-pack of yoghurts, and two crème fraiches. Although Mum is thinking of giving James a glass of vile soya a week. She claims he has been far less aggressive since the changeover. I said it was more to do with the fact that Keanu has been off school with alleged meningitis for several weeks. Apparently Mrs O'Grady and Dr Braithwaite (huge hands, lazy eye, bottle of whisky in desk drawer) are not as quick to spot purple Crayola as Mum.

Have got band practice after school. Tonight we are devoting several hours of rehearsal to choosing our outfits. It is a key decision. Look at David Bowie whose fame was entirely based on a shiny catsuit.

Thursday 26

Two days to go. Justin and I have agreed to forsake snogging for the sake of artistic endeavour. It was Scarlet's idea—she and Trevor are also abstaining for the rest of the week. She says it is like boxers not being allowed to do it before a big fight. It might detract from our performance.

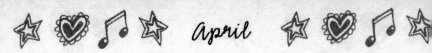

Saw Jack at Scarlet's after school. I said shouldn't he be rehearsing, instead of watching the Kerrang channel. He said, on the contrary, Kerrang is entirely educational, band-wise, and anyway, the Jack Stone Five were booked in for practice in the Jockey Wilson suite at 8 p.m. in order to check the acoustics and maximize their chances of clinching the title. I accused him of cheating but he said it is not cheating it is just cleverness. It is cheating. Justin agrees. He is sneaking The Back Doors in after over-50 aerobics tomorrow so they are not at a disadvantage. I asked Scarlet if we should go but she says our lyrics and composition will shine through like a beacon in the night and anyway, no one sounds that good in a room with sticky carpet and portraits of fat darts players on the walls.

Friday 27

School has gone Battle of the Bands mad. It is after the *Walden Chronicle* announced that one of the prizes is a support slot on a mystery tour this summer. The corridors of John Major High are now awash with rumours of who the headline act are. Fat Kylie claims it is 50 Cent as Mr Whippy heard it off 'ace' reporter Glen Davies when he was buying a Feast on the common last week. The goths are going for Spear of Destiny, whose drummer once drove through Saffron Walden, while the Alternative Music Table are crossing their fingers for a reformed Led Zeppelin.

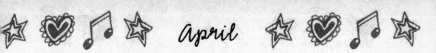
9 p.m.

Am home from final band practice. Scarlet has blessed her guitar and my voice with a vial of goth blood (fake vegetarian from Toys 'R' Us) and says our fate is now in the hands of supreme beings (she does not believe in God, only in Dracula). It is a shame the supreme beings include Hugo Thorndyke, evil Tory MP for Saffron Walden and environs. There is no way he is going to vote for Scarlet. Her parents are Labour councillors and sex workers. (Not in the prostitute sense though. Although Suzy would probably do quite well at that too.) Texted Justin to wish him luck. He says he does not need luck. He has the spirit of Jim Morrison in his fingers. He has also instructed me to be waiting backstage after the gig for resumption of full groupie duties. Am not sure I want Jim Morrison's fingers anywhere though. It is a bit weird.

Am not texting Jack. He will be too busy with his idiotic groupie. Hopefully it will sap all his artistic energy and he will be rubbish on stage tomorrow.

10 p.m.

Just got text from Jack. GD LUCK, RILEY. X. Have not texted back. It is probably a joke and Sophie is laughing at me this very minute. Thank goodness I am not hung up on him any more but am with love of my life. Otherwise I might have spent hours pondering the significance of that X.

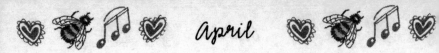
11 p.m.

But what if Sophie wasn't there and the X is actually a kiss and he actually cares whether I win or not?

11.15 p.m.

Which is question I do not need to know the answer to. As only care about Xs from Justin.

Saturday 28

8 a.m.

Hurrah. It is Battle of the Bands day. By this time tomorrow me and Scarlet could be lying on the floor of the Hawley Arms in Camden (essential hangout for drunken and drug-crazed celebrities). Excellent. I cannot wait. Have not told Mum this news yet. She will worry too much about my GCSEs and not having anything to fall back on. In fact have not even told her am in Battle of Bands. Am claiming I am going round Scarlet's for a Science revision party. She thinks we are going to play name that annelid. If I win it will be like that bit in *Dirty Dancing* and Justin can say, 'No one puts Rachel in a corner,' and I will stun them with my musical skills. Although she will probably not even notice I am gone anyway as Jesus has arrived for his custody visit. Treena dropped him off at half seven with a Teletubby, a bag of nappies, and a six pack of Wotsits. I checked for any wistfulness in her expression as she handed him over to

Grandpa but she just said, 'Watch him, Ern. He's eaten a shitload of grapes.'

Am taking my stage outfit to work and will get changed in the lentil storeroom. Do not know how I am going to get through eight hours of Mr Goldstein and Rosamund though. At least Justin gets to take his adrenalin out on chuck steak.

Wish me luck, dear diary. My next entry could be as Britain's next biggest export, after the Beckhams and tractors.

Sunday 29

10 a.m.
Head hurts. Not sure why. Will investigate in mirror.

Have huge bruise on side of head and what looks like chewing gum stuck in hair. But no idea how it got there. In fact cannot remember Battle of the Bands at all. Oh God. Am like Edward Norton in *Fight Club*. Maybe I have an insane alter ego that looks like Brad Pitt. Or possibly Angelina Jolie, in my case. That would be excellent. Will call Scarlet to see if I was behaving oddly last night.

10.15 a.m.
Am not like the one in *Fight Club*. Apparently it is due to Sophie Jacobs knocking me out with Scarlet's guitar after our rendition of 'Is She Really Going Out With Him?'

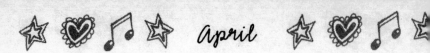
Asked Scarlet for summary of events at the Jockey Wilson Suite. They are as follows:

8 p.m.
The Back Doors give seminal performance, marred only by Sad Ed insisting on wearing dark glasses and not being able to see a lot of his keyboard.

8.15 p.m.
Jack Stone Five also give excellent performance. Fans go wild for Tuesday singing 'WLDN', as do judges, who are thinking of adopting it as theme tune to encourage more tourism.

8.30 p.m.
Velvet Elvis walk on stage.

8.34 p.m.
Trevor Pledger exits Jockey Wilson Suite in swish of voluminous goth cape, having taken offence at 'Bad Bat Boy and the Skinny Jeans'.

8.38 p.m.
Rachel Riley falls off stage after being thwacked with a Fender by Sophie Jacobs. Jack and Justin swarm stage to end potential bitch fight but end up wrestling on carpet tiles in actual battle of bands. Rachel carried to medical area (roller skate store) and handed to expert St John's Ambulance

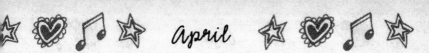
volunteer Roland McCafferty (high waist jeans (and not in a *Vogue* way), centre parting, snorkel jacket).

8.45 p.m.
Velvet Elvis, The Back Doors, and Jack Stone Five all disbarred from Battle of Bands for bringing competition into disrepute.

9 p.m.
Roland declares Rachel is concussed, not brain-damaged, and needs to go home to rest. Scarlet suggests Roland take her there in St John's ambulance. Roland points out that St John does not actually own ambulance and that he got a lift to the Lord Butler on the back of his brother's racer.

9.15 p.m.
Rachel ferried back to Summerdale Road by Bob in sick-smelling Volvo who informs Mum I have passed out due to excess revision. Amazingly, she believes him. Thank God Scarlet's parents are born liars and drug-takers.

10 p.m.
The Hermit Crabs, who Tippex their teeth and sing Beach Boys covers, win Battle of the Bands. Their prize is a tour of the Great Yarmouth area with someone called Bobby Helmet.

Oh God. Just had thought. What if Justin read too much into the lyrics. What if he has chucked me but I have blocked out the memory?

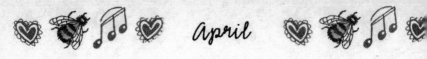
2 p.m.

Justin has rung. Obviously he did not read anything into lyrics. Possibly did not even understand lyrics at all. Thank God he is not intellectual marvel. I said it was totally cool that he rushed to my rescue against evil Sophie Jacobs and he is obviously utterly modest because then he went all quiet. I love him even more. Asked if he was coming to see me later but he said he is grounded over the fight with Jack for a week. He is my hero. I do not care that Velvet Elvis did not win the Battle of the Bands. My prize is greater—it is true love.

9 p.m.

Jack has just been round. Which was totally weird. He said he had come to check I was OK after the fight. I said I was fine, no thanks to his insane girlfriend. He said, 'Well, thanks for writing a song about me. I didn't know you cared.' I said I don't and anyway it wasn't about you it was about important themes of compatibility and politics. He said I am in denial. And I made an excellent joke about denial being a river in Egypt and I definitely saw him smile but then he said it's a shame it was me not your boyfriend who carried you to the medical room. Which is weird. As Justin didn't tell me that. So I said maybe he was in shock and too traumatized to carry me. But Jack said he was too busy talking to Sophie in the badminton changing rooms. I said that was a total lie so Jack said, 'Where is he now then?' I pointed out that he is grounded, thanks to his fight with

Jack. But Jack said, 'Whatever, that's why I saw him hanging around Pleasant Valley earlier.' Which is where Sophie lives. Then I didn't know what to say so I didn't say anything. And Jack came and sat next to me on the M&S duvet and said, 'Are you OK, Riley?' And I still didn't say anything so he held my hand. Then we just sat there for five minutes until 'Back to Black' got stuck on my CD player and I had to get up to stop Amy Winehouse saying 'rehab, rehab, rehab' repeatedly. Then Jack got up too. He said, 'Do me a favour. Don't tell Sophie I was here.' I said, 'As if. We don't even speak the same language.' (Which is totally a line from *The Breakfast Club* but sounded excellent here.) Then he went.

And now am totally confused. Why didn't Justin take me to the medical room when I could have been dead for all he knew? And why was he lurking near Sophie's if he is grounded? And why does Jack care anyway? Oh God, it is worse than GCSEs as there aren't even multiple choice answers. Am racked with indecision.

10 p.m.
Am unracked. Have had brilliant thought. It was not Justin on Pleasant Valley but was malodorous lesbian Oona Rickets. She has similar hair and men's shoes and was probably trying to sway Sophie to the 'other side'. Yes, that is it. It doesn't explain the rest of it, i.e. the lack of concern at my impending death, but at least it proves he is not a liar. Am glad Battle of the Bands is over. It has brought nothing but conflict to Saffron Walden.

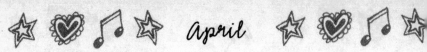
Monday 30

School is still obsessed with Battle of the Bands. Apparently rumours have reached such epic proportions that most of Year Seven thought I was languishing in intensive care in Addenbrookes with a plectrum lodged in my brain. Ms Hopwood-White had started a collection to pay for my wheelchair. On plus side, Justin and I are back as John Major High celebrity couple and no one is speaking to Sophie. Asked Scarlet how these ridiculous rumours started. She said Sad Ed.

Scarlet and Trevor are still not talking though. It has thrown Goth Corner Mark II into chaos. The boy goths are all backing Trevor for his hardline anti-EMO stance, but the girl goths, who see the attraction in colours other than black and purple, are behind Scarlet. Mrs Brain had to separate them at lunchtime with an overcooked Foccacia. She has designated a Goth Corner Mark III for Trevor and his bat friends next to the povvy table (aka Free School Dinners table). Scarlet is delighted as it is infinitely inferior to Goth Corner Mark II.

Have not mentioned my previous doubts to Justin. It is because, according to *Cosmopolitan*, love is all about trust. And sex. But mostly trust. And if I do not trust him totally we are doomed anyway so might as well not say anything. It is total *Catch-22*.

I'm RACHEL RILEY
– welcome to my so-called life.

May

Tuesday 1

Saw Jack on the way to school. He said, 'You still with Justin?' I said, 'You still with Sophie?' He said, 'Just.' I said, 'That's good.' He said, 'Yeah.' For someone who wants to be a politician he is not very good with words.

Wednesday 2

Velvet Elvis have officially broken up. Me and Scarlet have decided to concentrate on our GCSEs for a bit before conquering the music scene. Scarlet made the announcement in the canteen at lunch. Goth Corner Mark II and the Alternative Music Club table Mark I are in mourning. Unlike Goth Corner Mark III (i.e. Trevor's table) which is having a goth celebration of chewy fang sweets and blood (Ribena) to mark the occasion. Have told Justin I will be able to devote myself utterly to groupie duties from now on.

6 p.m.
Oh God, have just had awful thought. The *Walden Chronicle* comes out tomorrow. What if there are gruesome paparazzi shots of my injuries? Mum still doesn't know I was even at the Jockey Wilson suite. She has been spot-testing me on the periodic table all week. Have only got three out of ten. Unlike James who got 100 per cent. And in song. He says I

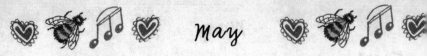
am looking at a D grade if I am lucky, and I had better pull my socks up.

Thursday 3

Sad Ed is on tenterhooks. It is because Edie has her first desperate housewife-style matchmaking date tonight with PC Doone. If all goes well Edie will be 'feeling the force' by eleven o'clock and will utterly not have to leave Saffron Walden and break up Tuesday and Sad Ed's love-across-a-divide relationship.

4 p.m.

Thank God. The notoriously ineffectual and reactionary *Walden Chronicle* has completely covered up the Battle of the Bands scandal. Instead the cover features a photo of the Hermit Crabs superimposed next to Bobby under the headline 'Helmet Catches Crabs'. Scarlet is outraged. She says it is like *Pravda*. I said, hardly. It is more like Primark. She said, '*Pravda*, not Prada, you heathen. It is an evil Russian propaganda newspaper. Like the *Daily Mail*. Which you would know if you had at all revised history.' Am definitely going to revise tonight. There was a blurry crowd shot of the Jockey Wilson suite inside, in which you can just see my science experiment jeans sprawled across the floor. But no one will be able to identify me from that.

4.15 p.m.

Mum has just demanded proof that I was revising at Scarlet's on Saturday night. She has been studying the *Walden Chronicle* with her magnifying glass gadget and says she is ninety-nine per cent sure those are my chemically enhanced jeans under the pool table. Have texted Scarlet. Suzy is always happy to lie.

4.30 p.m.

Suzy has just called Mum to check I enjoyed myself at the Science revisionathon. She says she personally kept a very strict eye on us and that we did not even turn the telly on once. I think she may have pushed it a bit. Mum will never believe that.

4.45 p.m.

Mum has called Suzy back to say her version of events on Saturday is flawed as there is a woman in the top left of the photo on page twenty-seven who looks exactly like Suzy i.e. heaving bosoms and not much clothing. Suzy immediately launched evasive tactics by pretending to have a bad line then hanging up. Mum has now grounded me for a week and banned me from any so-called revision parties at Scarlet's for ever on the grounds that Suzy cannot be trusted. I said she did not have incontrovertible proof that it was me or Suzy in the picture. She said she is happy to carry out forensic checks on my clothing for evidence of cider and passive smoking. I declined. She can sniff out teenage debauchery at twenty paces. I will accept my punishment

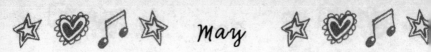
gracefully and use the time to better myself. Also as Justin is grounded it does not matter. We can just talk to each other on our phones. It will be like phone sex. Except about Jim Morrison and guitar strings, rather than sex. Obviously.

Friday 4

Sad Ed is depressed again. Edie and PC Doone did not hit it off over vegetarian moussaka. Instead Edie binge-ate Nigella's whisky and marmalade pudding in a bid to get drunk and escape PC Doone going on about his truncheon (his actual one, not the outsized one Suzy hoped he was referring to, which it turns out is not outsized—Suzy 'accidentally' walked in on him in the bathroom). So Tuesday is facing repatriation once again and Sad Ed is facing a lifetime of abstinence. I said what does it matter if he is dying soon anyway. But he said that is not the point. He wants to enjoy as many vices as possible during his few moments left. I asked what other vices he was enjoying, given Mrs Thomas's strict regime? He said gambling and drink. He means the lottery and the half a pint of shandy Suzy bought him at the gig.

Saturday 5

Nuts In May has been thrown into turmoil by some devastating news. Moonchild, i.e. ailment-ridden Rosamund,

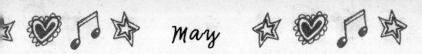

is leaving. She is moving in with Guru Derek at his chakra-healing compound in Steeple Bumpstead. Mr Goldstein is particularly hunched. It is the worry of finding a replacement. There are not many people who can stomach the smell of patchouli and liquorice root six days a week.

Scarlet is coming over later, as I am not allowed out into the free world. We are going to actually revise this time. She is bringing a DVD of Simon Scharma. She says it covers the entire history syllabus.

10 p.m.

Have not actually watched DVD but have absorbed information from the blurb on the cover. It is because we had important business to attend to, i.e. the Trevor situation. Scarlet is undecided as to whether or not to go back out with him. He has agreed to be seen with her in her skinny jeans but has drawn the line at retro ruffle skirts and Dita Von Teese lipstick. She says she is not sure whether this is a bad thing i.e. it is masculine oppression denying her the right to self-expression etc. Or a good thing, i.e. that his devotion to the dark side is unwavering i.e. he is not an infidel (what would that be—a fidel?). We did not come to a conclusion because at that point the dog fell down the stairs and the screams woke up Jesus. James was trying to teach it to fly. It is part of his Ninja training. It is not working.

Texted Justin to see how he is coping at our separation. No answer as yet. He is probably too miserable to reply.

Sunday 6

There has been another shocking revelation in Saffron Walden. Treena was spotted coming out of the Queen Elizabeth last night with none other than her ex-husband Des. There is photographic evidence, as taken by Marjory, on her way home from Jenga Club. She and Mum should definitely go into the private investigation business, they would make a fortune. Grandpa is devastated. So is Mum. She was hoping to have ousted him and the dog by next week. Also, she is cross because it means Baby Jesus will be having contact with someone with a criminal record and a tattoo (both high up her banned list).

Still no reply from last night's text to Justin. Will text again in case he has committed suicide due to separation.

5 p.m.
No answer. Will try again in morning. If has committed suicide will not be able to do anything about it anyway.

9 p.m.
Am being remarkably calm considering Justin has possibly killed himself. Maybe I am one of those people who is excellent in a crisis and does not panic. I could be a hostage negotiator. Or the queen.

Monday 7
May Day (Bank Holiday UK and Rep. Ire.)

9 a.m.
Still no word from Justin. Have called Scarlet to tell her of possible Justin suicide. She says give it until midday and then inform police of death.

11 a.m.
No word still. Have called Sad Ed for more advice. He says I should be thankful that Justin will be at peace with himself now. Also he is annoyed at Justin stealing his untimely death thunder. He is thinking of bringing the timetable forward.

11.45 a.m.
Cannot take it any more. Have called police and told them that rock legend Justin Statham has taken his own life in the attic of his mock tudor mansion. They asked if I had seen the body? I said not technically. They said how technically? I said it was just a hunch. They said they do not work on hunches. I said the woman out of *Murder She Wrote* did and she got it right 100 per cent of the time. They have agreed to send someone round. They do not want to be outdone by an eighty-year-old woman in comfortable footwear.

2 p.m.
Justin has just rung to complain about the police disturbing his bank holiday lie-in. Apparently he got woken by an

Alsatian licking his hair. It turns out he has not committed suicide. He has repetitive strain injury from an all-weekend Xbox marathon and his text thumb is only just recovering. He said I sounded very calm considering he was potentially dead. I said on the contrary I had been on the verge of flinging myself into the Slade in a suicide pact (not true but it sounds good). He said, 'You could have just rung.' This is true. Why did I not think of that? Anyway it is excellent that he is alive. I will value him all the more now.

Tuesday 8

Mr Vaughan has reminded us that we are supposed to be performing our Drama GCSE pieces next week in preparation for the external examiner next month. He said he hoped that they are all well on the way to curtain up readiness. Did not inform him that have yet to actually choose monologue. Though it is not hard to decide. Obviously will do tragic heroine i.e. Juliet, as I am practically her i.e. my family and Justin's are from different sides of the tracks (i.e. Debden Road) and we practically committed suicide in a tragic pact at the weekend. Sad Ed has already picked his. He is doing Othello. Though I think he may be asking the examiner to suspend their disbelief a little too far. He is neither dynamic nor black.

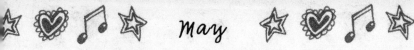
Wednesday 9

Grandpa's moping has reached new heights. He says he is too old for all this hoo-ha, that Treena has already rejected him because of his shrivelled thingy, and Mum will throw him out next like past-its-sell-by-date cheese and then no woman will have him. It is having a bad effect on the dog as well. It is lounging around in a most un-Ninjalike fashion, eating toffee and sighing every so often. Am going to call Suzy immediately and get Grandpa moved to the top of Edie's prospective lover list.

5 p.m.
Suzy says she is going to check with Edie to see if she has an upper age limit.

7 p.m.
Suzy says Edie will push sixty-five tops. I lied and said Grandpa was sixty-four.

7.15 p.m.
The hot date is confirmed. Grandpa is having dinner with Edie at Suzy's on Friday. Grandpa is now in a panic. He says there is no way he can pass for under seventy due to his white hair and droopy man-breasts. I said there was nothing I can do about man-breasts (gross) but that he should purchase some Grecian 2000 tomorrow and revive a natural, youthful look. He has agreed. Am excellent matchmaker.

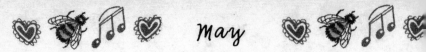
Like Barbra Streisand in *Hello, Dolly*, but without hideous perm, big nose, and vast dresses.

Thursday 10

Grandpa has purchased Grecian 2000. But is not natural light brown shade. Is black. I said he was supposed to be returning to his natural colour. He said I didn't specify whose natural colour. So I asked whose he was going for. He said Robert de Niro in *Taxi Driver*. He is thinking of doing the dog as well. He said it might cheer it up.

7 p.m.

Grandpa does not look like Robert de Niro. He looks like an ageing pervert. So does the dog. It is embarrassing. Grandpa is delighted though and is strutting round the house saying, 'You talking to me?' a lot. Mum is livid as all the beige M&S towels have indelible purple streaks on them. It is because the dog caught sight of itself in the mirror during the dye process and had a panic attack.

Friday 11

Am in trouble. Dad got his mobile phone bill from Wainwright and Hogg today. It turns out it is not paid automatically by direct debit and his personal calls are

not all free. He owes them £378. I said maybe his phone had been intercepted by French rat boys. But Mum dialled one of the suspicious numbers and got Justin who said, 'All right, Riley?' Mum said she was Mrs Riley to him and was not all right at all, and hung up. The bill has been added to the money I still owe her for the Desdemona hoo-ha. According to my calculations will still be paying debt off at Christmas unless I get a substantial pay rise from Mr Goldstein. Am definitely going to write to the Prime Minister to complain about poverty pay. And mobile phone tariffs. How are teenagers supposed to cope with the escalating cost of living? It is no wonder so many of us turn to glue or BBC3.

6 p.m.

Grandpa is dressed for his date. He is wearing a brown suit, last seen in 1960, and a pair of trainers that he got off Ducatti Mick for £10. He says he got the idea for his look off *Doctor Who*. I said yes but *Doctor Who* is not a seventy-five-year-old with black wig look and man-breasts. Even James is against it all. He says Grandpa is making a fool of himself. Plus he is annoyed as the hair dye is ruining the dog's training. Every time it walks past a window it goes bonkers and flings itself at the strange reflection. Mum has demanded to know where Grandpa is going dressed like an Eastern European. He said he has a date with destiny. Thank God he did not say Edie. She would have banned him from leaving the house for sure.

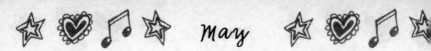

11 p.m.

Grandpa is back. Apparently the *Doctor Who* look worked as he and Edie are meeting on Sunday for a second date. Asked how far he had gone on the first date. He said to the second door on the right. Have no idea what it means.

Saturday 12

Have got a broken finger due to being on Nuts In May till duty all day today. It is because Mr Goldstein was in the stockroom conducting interviews for Moonchild's old job. I suggested he should be looking for someone young and dynamic to bring Nuts In May into the twenty-first century. He said he was quite happy in the current century (i.e. the nineteenth in his case) and to get back on the shop floor as lentils do not sell themselves. He is wasting an opportunity. If he got rid of the Beanfeast display he could add a computer and be a health food internet café so that people could Google their many symptoms and drink nettle tea before purchasing homeopathic so-called cures. I should be on *The Apprentice*. I am definite thrusting entrepreneurial type.

Unlike the candidate list which consisted of:

- Mrs Noakes from WHSmith (no chin; bad perm; calls trousers 'slacks') who is only thinking of changing job because it gives her more chance to observe potential

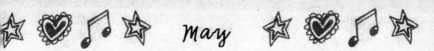
drug-users and deviants (hippy types and teenagers buying Buzz Gum).

- Mrs Goldstein (Unlikely to get job as Mr Goldstein says she is too meddling. Dad would sympathize here. Mum once applied to Wainwright and Hogg and Dad intercepted the form and burnt it. Mum still thinks she was turned down on the grounds that she was overqualified).

- Mrs Thomas (i.e. Sad Ed's mum. She says she needs to start saving for Sad Ed's college education. Did not tell her he is hoping to be dead before graduation).

Mr Goldstein is giving the job to Mrs Thomas. He said she is exactly the right sort of person Nuts In May needs i.e. old and averse to change. Except that she can't do Saturdays due to her many Aled Jones Fan Club fixtures so now Mr Goldstein needs a new Saturday girl. Have suggested Scarlet. Then we can use potentially wasted hours working to discuss ongoing Trevor crisis.

Met Justin behind meat bins as usual for snogging/lunch. I said it is excellent that tonight is my last night of being grounded i.e. watching *Casualty* with Mum and Dad when I could be usefully watching it at Justin's. He said, 'Mmm.' His mouth was full of scotch egg at the time so I expect he meant, 'I cannot wait to spend Saturday night in your loving arms again.' It is a known fact that absence makes the heart grow fonder. He must be bursting with love for me by now.

Sunday 13

Am devoting the day to perfecting my performance as Juliet. Justin is coming over later to be the audience and am aiming to stun him into flinging me on the Lenor-scented duvet and snogging me within an inch of my life. Although am under strict instructions to leave bedroom door open at all times for anti-sex spot checks.

Grandpa is devoting the day to his performance as Robert de Niro/*Doctor Who* with Edie as his audience. They are taking Jesus and the dog out for a romantic walk on the common. I said it might be better to leave Jesus and/or the dog at home if he was hoping for romance but he says he wants Edie to see him warts and all (he is not being entirely metaphorical, he actually has warts). Also he needs them as cover for Mum. She will be suspicious if he goes out unaccompanied. He is making a mistake. Edie absolutely should not be seeing Grandpa's warts at this stage of their relationship. She will dump him within minutes. Although at least he will not have Mum or James checking that he is not touching proscribed zones every five minutes.

5 p.m.
Romantic walk not quite as planned. Apparently things began to unravel when they bumped into Treena and Des at the swings. Grandpa took his whole timelord/gangster thing too seriously and launched himself at

Des in a frenzied attack. Des is now in Addenbrookes with a bleeding ear. It is not from Grandpa. Or the dog, who refused to follow the command to 'kill' as it was too busy spinning on the roundabout. It is from Treena. Apparently she and Edie share similar tastes in crap hair dye and 1960s nylon suits as she got all wistful about Grandpa's youthful look and took a swing at Des with her handbag.

Grandpa and Treena have gone for immediate summit talks at the Queen Elizabeth. Edie brought the dog and Baby Jesus home.

Also am excellent Juliet. Justin definitely impressed. Did not exactly fling himself at me with abandon, but said it was very 'emotional'. It is the special crying effect—thanks to Vicks inhaler rubbed under eyes. Tried to summon up depressing memories in method acting style but nothing tragic has happened to me yet so have had to resort to artificial means.

Monday 14

Grandpa has gone back to the bosom of his family. Treena says that Des was a just a sex thing and Grandpa is her ONE. Yes and Grandpa is not on probation which helps. The dog is still here though. Treena says it is a condition of their reconciliation. I am amazed she didn't try to leave Jesus as well.

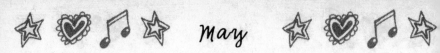
5 p.m.

Oooh. Maybe Edie will get together with Des. He could be her bit of rough. He has excellent credentials including GBH and attempted armed robbery. Will call Suzy immediately and suggest it.

5.15 p.m.

Edie says she will try Des but that she is hoping to get Mr Vaughan in next as she thinks he may be the one due to his former (and possibly current) drug habit.

Tuesday 15

Had horrid shock at breakfast. Have dentist appointment with sadistic Mrs Wong at eleven. Mum says it is nil by mouth until then. I begged for some nerve-fortifying Marmite on toast but Mum says she does not want Mrs Wong complaining about crumbs in my molars. On plus side I will miss French i.e. two hours of Mark Lambert trying to pronounce '*l'hôpital*'.

4 p.m.

Oh God. Have horrifying news. Mrs Wong says I have to wear a brace. Am going to look like Danny Stanton in Year Eight aka Jaws. Justin will not want to snog me in case he gets lacerated on the metal bits. And will have bits of lettuce stuck in them all the time. Am going to be social

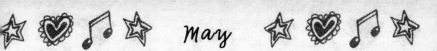

pariah and virgin for rest of life. Or at least for six months. Though Mum has agreed to delay fitting until after GCSEs to lessen my trauma. She is worried it may cause a speech impediment and interfere with my French oral.

Also saw Emily Reeve in waiting room looking fat and nervous. It is because all your teeth fall out when you are pregnant. At least that's what Granny Clegg claims is the cause of several of her missing teeth.

5 p.m.
Mum says it was not pregnancy that made Granny Clegg's teeth drop out. It was drinking tins of condensed milk.

Wednesday 16

Mr Vaughan said my Juliet was promising. If a little overwrought. He says a bit less crying would help. It is because I overdid the Vicks Vapour Rub in my enthusiasm. Was still crying in Rural Studies. Cowpat Cheesmond had to send me to Mrs Leech with suspected 'girls' trouble'. She gave me a tissue and a bourbon biscuit and said, 'They are all bastards.' I just nodded through my mentholated tears.

Also Mr Vaughan is refusing to go out with Edie. It is the age difference. (He is not so fussy when it is the other way around.) So is Barry the Blade. He says it is not the age but that he is in love with white-flare-wearing wee-smelling Mrs Simpson. Although she is in love with dead gay singer

May

Freddie Mercury. She claims his spirit lives in her airing cupboard and is dictating a novel to her. She is planning to sell it and make millions, once Freddie has finished. Suzy asked Barry what the story is about. It is about a dead singer who lives in an airing cupboard.

Sad Ed says he is doomed to singledom. I said if his relationship was as rock solid as mine and Justin's then he has nothing to fear. He said, 'Oh, great.'

Thursday 17

8.30 a.m.
Oh God. Think may have been dumped. Fat Kylie has just texted me to ask if I want Mr Whippy to duff Justin up. She says he will happily 'stick his ice cream scoop where the sun don't shine'. What is going on? Am going to text Scarlet.

8.35 a.m.
Scarlet says Jack says that Sophie heard he was going to dump me but was waiting until after my exams in case Mum blamed him for me failing. (He is right. She would do.) Oh God. It is utterly tragic. I am single and he doesn't even have the heart to tell me himself. It is totally like *Pretty in Pink* where Blane is too embarrassed to admit he does not want to take Andy to the prom because she is poor and wears second-hand clothes and her dad is jobless and wears vests (not under things, like Dad, but as actual clothes).

9 a.m.

Am not dumped. It is just a vicious rumour started by security-unconscious Mrs Leech due to the Vick's Vapour Rub incident. Justin says he would not chuck me just before my GCSEs. That would be cruel and heartless. He is so thoughtful. I am lucky to have him.

Sad Ed is happy too. He and Tuesday have come up with a new plan to keep Edie in Saffron Walden. They have signed her up for driving lessons in a bid to give her something to aim for in life. And to stop Tuesday having to rely on Mr Wilmott and his car of shame (i.e. the Vauxhall Cavalier) turning up to collect her.

Friday 18

Treena has rung to invite me to her thirtieth birthday party tomorrow. Asked her who was going. She said her cousin Donna (who is 'totally mental') and some of the old ladies from the Twilight Years Day Centre (the continent and mobile ones). Asked if I could bring anyone. She said yes but it is girls only so that they can watch *Dirty Dancing* and leer at Patrick Swayze without having to turn over for *Match of the Day*. Am going to take Scarlet. She is all for female caucus things. She says it is an essential demonstration of sisterhood. It is more likely to be a demonstration of tequila drinking in Treena and Donna's case. Have told Justin that I am 'out with the girls'. He did

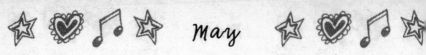
not seem too disappointed. It is because he totally trusts me and is secure in us having our own interests and time apart. (I learnt that off Suzy. I also learnt some horrible facts about penises, which I cannot even bear to write down.)

Saturday 19

Am sick of being on till. Now have bleeding knuckles which is not good look for party. Luckily Suzy came into shop (to purchase incense sticks to cover up a burning cat-hair smell—Edna has singed Gordon with a Rothman's) and told her to remind Scarlet to offer herself up for work immediately before I actually lose a limb. Also reminded her to tell Scarlet to meet me at 19 Harvey Road at eight o'clock precisely as do not want to be left alone with Treena and her girl gang for too long. Jesus is round ours already. He is riding the dog up and down the stairs. So is Grandpa. (Round our house, I mean, not riding the dog. That would be impossible, not to mention probably illegal.) They have had a lucky escape. I fear Treena's all-girl thirtieth will descend into anarchy and shrieking before Patrick has even taken his shirt off. Or maybe turning thirty will mark a new and thoughtful period in Treena's life. Now that she is middle-aged and a mother and wife.

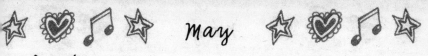

May

Sunday 20

Oh God. Have seen Mark Lambert's dad's willy (aka Mr Hosepipe's hosepipe). Think that is definitely illegal. It is because Donna hired him to be the fireman strippergram. Though at least have not touched it. Which is more than I can say for Elsie Stain (eighty-nine, four foot seven, false teeth which clack and fall out when she gets overexcited, which is a lot).

Party was as predicted i.e. anarchy and shrieking. It is because Treena invited the neighbours, i.e. Fat Kylie, who ignored the girls only rule and brought with her not just Thin Kylie and some female O'Gradys (Mrs and Paris-Marie) but also all the male ones too (Stacey, Dane, Finbarr, and Kyle plus two others I have never seen before, both called Liam). At least she left Keanu and Whitney at home. She did not bother with a babysitter. The walls are paper-thin and you can hear the screams even over Jennifer Warnes at full volume. Drank only Red Bull so as to avoid another O'Grady snogging fiasco. Scarlet should have followed my restrained example. She drank four cans of Carlsberg and ended up snogging one of the Liams (not sure which, they both have the same look of Celtic menace). It is lucky I was sober and also strengthened by excess caffeine intake as managed to prise them apart and drag her to safety (i.e. Summerdale Road) before anything else happened. She is still asleep on floor in my Millets sleeping bag. Have followed Mum's example and put bucket and Cillit Bang

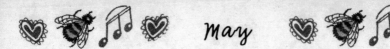

next to her head in case of vomit. She looks peaceful. It will be sad to have to wake her and impart the news that I am no longer alone in my shame and that she too has swapped saliva with an O'Grady.

11 a.m.
Scarlet still snoring. Am actually quite jealous as only got two hours sleep due to excess Red Bull. Ended up manically solving quadratic equations until five in morning.

12 noon
Scarlet still asleep.

1 p.m.
Have woken Scarlet up as do not want to miss Sunday lunch. Told her terrible news and asked if she would be ending it with Trevor forthwith. She says on the contrary, it has only confirmed her true love for Trevor. She feels renewed in their relationship, and in her goth vows, and is going round there now to offer herself up to his goth mercy (after she has showered all traces of O'Grady off herself, obviously).

Monday 21

Scarlet and Trevor are officially back together. Goth Corner Mark II is a haven of peace and bat toys once

again. Scarlet says they are going to allow each other their freedom to wear whatever clothes they want. (Except Tommy Hilfiger. Even I would draw the line there.) She also said this time they are going to be utterly honest with each other and tell each other everything. Asked if she had confessed about the O'Grady liaison. She said no.

Tuesday 22

Mum and Dad are sulking again. It is because Dad is annoyed as it took him two hours to get home from work this evening due to a car crash. Mum is not annoyed that he is late. She is annoyed because the crash involved a Ford Fiesta wedged across one of the myriad mini-roundabouts. Dad is blaming Fiestas for a persistent steering fault. Mum has countered by quoting Passat crash statistics. James is now acting as official statistician to both sides and is Googling evidence as I write.

8 p.m.

It gets worse. Sad Ed has rung. The crash was no ordinary Fiesta. It was one of Mike 'Wandering Hands' Majors's driving school fleet. And at the wheel was none other than Edie. The news has not gone down well with Mum. She says Edie is sabotaging Dad from afar by stopping him getting home in time for his liver and onions. Not only that but she

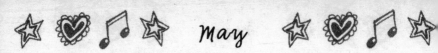

is putting a pillar of the community (i.e. Mike Wandering Hands) at risk of death from her inability to follow rules of any kind. Dad says the crash was probably due to Mike's wandering hands wandering too close to Edie. They are now watching *Top Gear* in strained silence. James has taken the dog upstairs. He says all the hoo-ha is not good for its Ninja sensitivities. Am inclined to agree. Although the dog is still not showing any potential as a superhero. This morning it fell in the toilet.

Wednesday 23

Saffron Walden is awash with rumours about Edie and Mike. Mum is livid. She says it will all be over by next week once he realizes she is a law-breaker. (Binge drinking is illegal in Mum's book. Which is an actual book. It is the one she uses to write down anti-social behaviour in.) I said she should be happy his wandering hands are occupied as it kills several birds with one stone. Mum says it is not Mike's hands she is worried about. It is his devotion to upholding the Highway Code. She thinks he will go all lax under Edie's malign influence.

Thursday 24

Sad Ed has confirmed Mike and Edie rumours. Apparently the near-death experience of wedging a Fiesta into a traffic

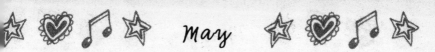

bollard has brought them closer together, literally and metaphorically. Vest-wearing Colin Riley is off the hook and Tuesday can remain a British citizen and girlfriend of Sad Ed, until his untimely death, that is. He is very pleased. Not only will he get regular sex until that event but he will have someone to weep hysterically and fling themselves on his grave at his funeral. In addition to Mrs Thomas.

Friday 25

12 noon

Hurrah. It is the last day of lessons for Year Eleven. I am another giant step closer to non-uniform wearing, black coffee drinking, uber-left-wing Sixth Form, with just the minor hurdle of an entire month of GCSEs to cross. Mr Wilmott herded everyone into the canteen for his annual motivational assembly, success rate negligible, since we are still languishing below the Burger King Sports Academy in the league tables. But this year he has an added incentive. Clearly Tuesday has been influencing him with her American ways because he has announced that there will be a 'prom' for Years Eleven to Thirteen. Am overwhelmed with potential *Pretty in Pink* excitement. Think will use occasion to abandon myself to Justin i.e. do 'It'. Although he has not pushed point for a while. If at all. I know will not be technically sixteen but will mark the end of my childhood, i.e. GCSEs, and anyway it

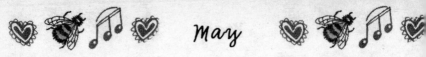

May

is practically compulsory to have done 'It' to be allowed entry into common room.

Mr Wilmott also announced elections for head boy and girl. All current Lower Sixth are eligible. Justin says no one in their right mind would want to be head boy as it means having to wear a crap badge (made by Mrs Leech and her Fisher Price badge making machine). Plus the only actual powers you get are patrolling the Retards and Criminals and telling them to stop breaking things. The campaigns will begin immediately after GCSEs end. Mr Wilmott says it is so we can give our full attention to the various manifestos and not just make rash judgements on looks (or smells in the case of Oona Rickets who is bound to stand). He is wasting his time. It will all come down to 'shagability'. The Maths Club have proved it with several correlation charts.

3 p.m.

Justin has put his name on the list for head boy. It is not because he has had a change of heart over the crap badge or minimal powers, it is because Jack and Sophie have signed up and he refuses to be beaten by Jack, even at things he does not want. I pointed out that he is leaving Sixth Form after retakes, but he says he has put in for emergency A level choices (PE, Music, and Drama). I said he must not give up his musical career for me, even though it is utterly romantic and almost like taking a bullet! He said he is not. It is because Braintree's Rock Foundation is under threat from a 'Mickey Mouse course' crackdown.

Saturday 26

Oh my God. Mr Goldstein has employed a new Saturday girl. Except it is not a girl. It is Jack. I demanded an employee conference immediately but Mr Goldstein said Jack was the only applicant and there was nothing to discuss, besides which he had gyppy hump and not to bother him. So I texted Scarlet to ask why she was not here and her treacherous brother was. But she was obviously too busy rediscovering Trevor's gothic bits as she did not reply.

It is utterly unfair. Especially as Mr Goldstein has let Jack have lunch at one and moved my lunch break to twelve, so Justin and I will have to forsake our meat bin snog. Maybe Jack is doing it on purpose to annoy me and Justin. He is definitely up to something. Am also worried he may be trying to oust me as top dog in Mr Goldstein's eyes. He has a vegetarian progressive sex guru mother who has a cabinet full of homeopathic cures. Whereas my mother is more acquainted with sausages and Tixylix.

9 p.m.
Told Justin about Jack situation after work. He said I should use it to our advantage, i.e. to wheedle potential campaign-shattering information out of him. I said that would be totally underhand and evil. He said exactly.

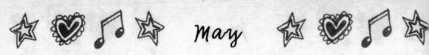
Sunday 27
Whit Sunday (Pentecost)

Granny Clegg has rung. The hip of doom is gyppy again. She says it is so painful it may be foretelling a whole mass of potential deaths. But Mum says she has had enough hip of doom hoo-ha and has ordered Granny to make an appointment with the doctor. Granny has agreed but says she will still be keeping an eye on the news for serial killers, mass salmonella poisonings, and train crashes.

Monday 28
Spring Holiday (UK)

9 a.m.

Think will start revision today. Although Suzy says it is essential to have relaxing 'you' time during this traumatic period. So maybe will watch a bit of TV and have brain-stimulating Shreddies first.

12 noon

Am utterly relaxed after *Friends* marathon. Will get down to history revision now. Although am bit hungry again. Will just eat vitamin-filled apple. And watch mind-expanding Channel 4.

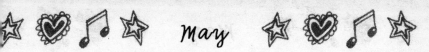
12.55 p.m.
Now will start.

1 p.m.
Oh. Lunchtime. Tuna sandwiches. Had better eat it as it is full of omega 3 which is essential exam-passing food.

2.30 p.m.
Am now tip-top brainwise. Oooh. Text from Sad Ed. His CD player is on blink and he cannot play 'The Best of Leonard Cohen' (a misnomer, it is all horrible) which means he cannot revise at home. He is coming over to hijack mine.

2.45 p.m.
Cannot revise with sound of mournful moaning in ear. (Leonard Cohen, not Sad Ed. Although he is quite annoying too as he keeps trying to sing along.) Will fetch digestives to shut him up and revise when Ed has gone.

6 p.m.
After tea obviously.

7 p.m.
Hmm. It is quite late and do not want to tax brain into having meltdown. Think will watch television and start tomorrow.

Tuesday 29

8.30 a.m.
Am totally ready for revision. Will just eat Shreddies and then will get down to it. James is uncharacteristically absent from the Shreddie table. He has taken a giant roll of paper, his set of 100 washable felt pens (actually ninety-nine and not washable, according to Mum, and now subject of pedant letter and potential lawsuit) and some stickers to his bedroom. It is obviously Ninja-related. He is probably drawing up a blueprint of the sewer for the dog to learn. He is wasting his time. The dog gets lost in the kitchen with the lights out.

9 a.m.
Maybe just need one episode of *Kensington Gore* to prepare mentally.

9.01 a.m.
Kensington Gore rudely interrupted by James with a patented, colour-coded, reward-based revision schedule. He says he cannot let me fritter my future away on cheap television (this is rich coming from someone who worships at the shrine of the Turtles) and is taking over as chief adviser during this essential period. Have pleaded with Mum to rescue me but she says she is backing him all the way. He is like her mini-me.

James says it is rigorous, but, on the plus side, it is easy to follow. It is divided into hourly timeslots from 7 a.m. to

6 p.m., with half an hour for lunch and ten minute breaks for digestives at eleven and three. Each subject has a different colour and I get a sticker for every hour successfully completed. He will also be conducting tests at the end of each day and, if I win, I get a *Lord of the Rings* figurine. He says it is a tried and tested carrot and stick method, with the stickers and action figures being the metaphorical carrots. Asked what the stick was. He said spending the rest of my life as one of the great uneducated of our family i.e. down a tin mine like Grandpa Clegg. Have agreed. Do not want to be in same mental bracket as pasty-waving moron.

7 p.m.
Am exhausted. But have won two orcs (History and Science). Only narrowly missed Gollum. (Rural Studies—chickens do not have a nine-month gestation period. They lay eggs. Complained that it was a trick question but James said it is like *Who Wants to be a Millionaire* and there are no trick questions, just stupid answers.)

Wednesday 30

7 p.m.
Have completed second day of Riley-patented exam method. Am totally going to beat Scarlet, who is following Suzy's 'exams aren't everything' mantra. She is doing two hours a day interspersed with yoga, hummus, and snogging

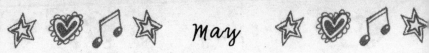

May

bat boy. I on other hand am too focused to snog Justin and have texted him to stay away during this crucial period. He does not care. He is hanging out at the Mocha trying to win over the key waster vote. Pointed out that he was supposed to be revising too but he says he did it all on Sunday.

Thursday 31

7 p.m.
Got a hobbit (French) and Legolas (English) today. Although James handed them over with a tear in his eye. It is not delight in my achievements. It is because the blonde one off *Blue Peter* is leaving. He says it is the end of an era. It is the end of him and Grandpa Riley ogling children's television.

Also Granny Clegg rang. Apparently (and predictably) Dr Kimber does not believe in the hip of doom. She says it is a hip of arthritis and needs replacing. Granny Clegg is now on the waiting list for a new, non-death-predicting one. Grandpa Clegg has told her not to worry, it will be years before the op and she has plenty of time to solve crime until then.

I'm RACHEL RILEY
— welcome to my so-called life.

June

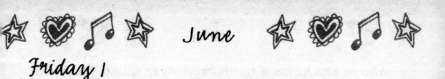
Friday 1

Am definite genius. Have completed all but two slots in James's chart (one due to dog-related bathroom fracas, and the other an overlong lunchbreak as it was Mum's goulash which is notoriously chewy) and passed seventy-five per cent of James's 'tough but fair' exam quizzes. Am now only missing Aragorn and that Liv Tyler one from *Lord of Rings* figurine collection. Though obviously will be giving them back to James as am *a*) not loser and *b*) he has made clear they are only on temporary incentivizing loan.

Saturday 2

No revision today due to actual work. Mum says I should give up for the duration of the exams but I said the maths needed to add up lentil bills and operate the till of death would be excellent revision. Also have worked out am still around £576 in debt due to death of Desdemona, Glastonbury ticket, Dad's phone bill, and having to repay Justin his £50 mobile minutes so cannot afford to give up. Was sweeping up muesli bits when Justin texted me to remind me to use my time at work to glean head boy information out of Jack. Decided to go for open, journalistic approach (as am excellent at it, as proven by brief career at *Walden Chronicle*) so asked him why he was standing for position. He says it is all good practice for when he is an anti-war foreign secretary.

Also he says he has a groundbreaking manifesto for a vastly improved Sixth Form, including a new sofa and a condom machine. Which I must admit does sound good. But had to be loyal so said he had no chance of winning now that Justin was in the running. Jack said no one will vote for Justin as he is utterly transparent and is only doing it to impress Sophie. I said didn't he mean me. He said, 'Yeah, right.' He was obviously slightly high from the overpowering smell of hemp oil. Or else he has Sophie Microwave Muffins on the brain. Anyway he is wrong. Everyone will vote for Justin. He is a living legend. And has lovely arms.

9 p.m.

Justin not impressed with information. (Although he says he may 'borrow' some of the manifesto ideas. Especially the new sofa, as one of the springs pierced his left-weave Gap jeans last week.) He says he wants dirt. Like sex secrets or skeletons in the cupboard. I said I did not think Jack had any skeletons in his cupboard. He said all politicians do so I asked him what his was. He said his mum once made him wear his sister's pants to school when she forgot to wash his. He is right. That sort of information could cost him the campaign if it was ever made public.

Sunday 3

Am having total GCSE panic. Is less than twenty-four

hours until I potentially seal my fate as literary genius or pie-serving shopgirl. Mum is not helping by pointing out that she got nine O levels all at Grades A and B. James asked Dad how many he got. He said not as many. James said how many. He said six. None at Grade A. And two of them were Woodwork and Metalwork. But that is not the point because exams were harder in those days and today his results would translate into at least eleven A*s. James agreed and said that modern GCSEs are not worth the paper they are written on. So I said I might as well not bother but then Mum intervened with her well-practised 'exams are the meaning of life' speech. (Which is sort of like the 'I have a dream' speech but with fewer references to black people. And more spoon-thrusting.) I said I thought sex was the meaning of life as without it we would all be dead. Mum said on the contrary exams are what separates the wheat from the chaff and in fact there ought to be an exam before anyone has sex, which in her opinion, neither I nor James, nor any of the O'Gradys would ever pass. Then James said we were both wrong and that in fact the meaning of life is '42'. So Mum sent us both to our rooms for questioning her version of events. She is like a creationist in her academic zeal.

Anyway she is wrong. Sex is the meaning of life. And once have finished GCSEs, will concentrate on passing next test i.e. doing 'It'.

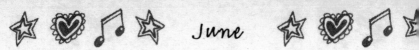

June

Monday 4
D-Day

8 a.m.

Am totally ready for first GCSE i.e. Maths. Have eaten special breakfast of boiled omega 3 eggs and Shredded Wheat with omega 3 milk (purchased by Mum in panic exam-passing bid).

8.15 a.m.

Scarlet has texted to make sure I have packed my lucky mascot. She is taking a mini Marilyn Manson and Sad Ed has got a toy rabbit called Frobisher. Oh God. Do not have lucky toy since dog ate Larry the lamb. Will have to borrow one off James.

8.18 a.m.

Am taking talking Madonna. It is the only one he is willing to part with except for a high fee, which I cannot afford due to scale of debt crisis. Have texted Justin special good luck message.

8.19 a.m.

Got special message back from Justin. 'TA, RILEY'. He is obviously too overwrought at thought of failing English for second time to send me good luck back. Will not worry about it. Will remember that in six weeks will be united with him in sexual ecstasy. Possibly.

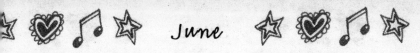

3 p.m.

Exam delayed by an hour due to lucky mascot issues. Mr Wilmott says calculators and revision folders do not qualify. Nor do live pets. This is because Davey MacDonald brought in his hamster Beckham which escaped and was last seen heading for Mrs Brain's canteen. It is obviously as mental as Davey MacDonald as no one goes there voluntarily. Mr Wilmott also questioned the talking Madonna. He is worried it may have been reprogrammed with exam answers. Offered to let him press her breasts to hear it in action. He did. It said, 'Like a virgin, touched for the very first time.'

Think have done OK though. Questions remarkably untaxing e.g. 'Five people like watching the *News*. Twelve people like watching *Police Chase*. How many more people like *Police Chase* than the *News*?' Even Mark Lambert cannot get that wrong. It is seven. Obviously. James is right. GCSEs are not worth the paper they are written on.

3.05 p.m.

Oh God. What if it was a trick question? Cannot think about it. It is too late. Have to get back to James's new exam time schedule (still colour-coded with stickers but without *Lord of Rings* figurines as he has run out of them since dog bit Aragorn's head off during *Antiques Roadshow* last night).

Tuesday 5

Have got English Lit. today. Which am not worried about as am practically literary marvel anyway.

3 p.m.
A cinch. Had to write about a weak character in *Of Mice and Men*. It is obviously the old man called Candy as he is ancient and shrivelled.

3.05 p.m.
Unless it was metaphorical. In which case the answer could have been giant moron. Anyway it does not matter as there are no right or wrong answers in English. Only opinions.

3.10 p.m.
Unless you are Fat Kylie and put down Smike who is not even in *Of Mice and Men*. That is not an opinion, that is just mentalism. At least is Science tomorrow. There is no opinion there, just fact.

Wednesday 6

Although if do not know facts then opinion would be easier. What, for God's sake, is immobilized lactase? Is English again tomorrow. Thank God.

Thursday 7

English Language rescheduled to Friday due to Retard-related incident in exam hall.

Friday 8

School shut due to lack of electricity. According to Mrs Leech, there is rodent damage in one of the fuse boxes. All fingers point to Beckham the lucky hamster. English rescheduled to Monday, along with French and Maths.

Scarlet has threatened to go on strike against the giant exam marathon but Mr Wilmott says if he leaves it any longer then criminal elements (he means O'Gradys and Mark Lambert) will get hold of the exam papers from the Burger King Sports Academy and cheating will be rife. Scarlet pointed out that this could raise his grade point average several marks and he did waiver for several seconds but has erred on the side of the law. Also, he underestimates the O'Gradys. They can get exam papers in one hour, via a web of loose-moralled motorcycle couriers operating in the Bishop's Stortford area, as testified to by Thin Kylie who sat Science in isolation an hour late on Wednesday due to an alleged brain tumour. So-called school nurse Mrs Leech checked her over for symptoms using a stethoscope from the Drama wardrobe department and a biology textbook. Thank God she is not an actual nurse. She diagnosed her

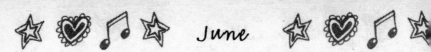
with rickets but said she could get treatment after the exam.

Am actually looking forward to work tomorrow. It will be welcome relief from general hothouse atmosphere. Also, saw Sophie lurking around Justin outside Mr Patel's. Am going to let him touch breast tomorrow night. It will lure him away from Sophie, even if it is a minuscule A cup. Not sure which one though. Maybe the right one as it is discernibly bigger, by at least three millimetres according to Scarlet.

Saturday 9

Breast touching did not go according to plan. Justin was concentrating on trying to make his hair look exactly like Jim Morrison's on the cover of eponymously titled album 'The Doors' so said I felt constricted and asked if he minded if I took my top off. But, and this was the cunning part, I was not wearing anything underneath except my bra. But somehow I got wound up in a sleeve and fell backwards and knocked a glass of Vimto over his turntable. So instead of groping my breast, he just said, 'Jesus, Riley. That's bloody vintage Zepp.' I pointed out there was also some dripping on the cream shagpile and said he should use Stain Devils but not the one for red wine, the one for ink. It is one of Mum's tried and tested tips.

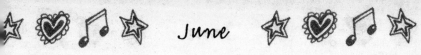
Sunday 10

Granny Clegg rang. The hip of doom has gone ominously silent. She thinks it could be something to do with Armageddon. She says Maureen at the Spar says her hairdresser says the world is going to end on Tuesday. Or possibly Friday. Mum said, thank God. It is because James has flooded the bathroom. He was trying to recreate a sewer-like atmosphere for the dog. Mum said he could have just taken him for a walk in the shopping-trolley-clogged Slade.

Monday 11

8.15 a.m.
Have had double omega 3 eggs in preparation for marathon exam day of Maths, French, and English Lang. Am fully revised and nothing can go wrong.

8.20 a.m.
Where is talking Madonna? Oh God. Am utterly going to fail if cannot locate lucky mascot.

8.30 a.m.
Madonna is missing, presumed in dog. It is feigning innocence but every so often there are faint snatches of an American accent from its general direction. James has

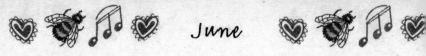

offered giant David Beckham cut-out or naked Prince William as a replacement. Neither look particularly lucky. Am going to depend on brain power instead. Lucky mascots are not actually lucky. It is all in the mind.

3 p.m.

Why, oh why, did dog eat talking Madonna? It is all his fault I could not concentrate in any exams. It is because Madonna has a calming presence and I can stare into her empty plastic eyes and the answers come springing to my mind. Today just had to stare at back of Fat Kylie's head which is utterly uninspiring and not at all calming due to gel to hair ratio.

Tuesday 12

Hurrah. Am totally going to pass English though. Had to write about a typical day in my household to show aliens what life in England is like. Was very informative including details of the various ongoing bans in force in the house (Ribena, ITV, E4, overusing the word 'like') although used artistic licence when describing James or they will think I am making him up. No one is that pedantic or weird in real life. The dog came off well too. I skirted around him eating Madonna and said it was a model of the US President. It makes me sound more politically aware and the dog possibly anti-war. Is Drama tomorrow. Am going to get into

the Juliet mood now and stay in character until tomorrow.
It is not hard as have utterly Capulet-like restrictive parents.
May get Justin to shout up at window later in a lovestruck
manner.

8 p.m.
Justin is refusing to pledge undying love for me down the
side of the garage. He is worried Mum will take umbrage
and throw something at him. He is right to be scared. She is
always flinging stuff at cats. And Thin Kylie.

Wednesday 13

Mum says I am taking the in-character thing too far. It is
because I refused omega eggs and demanded more Juliet-
like gruel. Got Ready Brek in end. With golden syrup. Even
Juliet would have had syrup on gruel. Stomach feels a bit
funny now though. It is nerves at exam. Or maybe have
become Juliet and it is love for Romeo!

10 a.m.
Think it is not love but possible overeating of Ready
Brek. Am doubled over in pain. But will soldier on like
professional.

3 p.m.
Mr Vaughan says my Juliet was fascinating, especially the

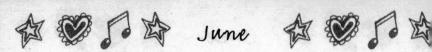

June

decision to play her as a hunchback. He says it was excellent planning to work with Mr Goldstein as research and will be lobbying the examiner to give me extra marks for this dedication to the art. Hurrah.

Thursday 14

Yet more Science. Which is hard and pointless. Who cares what the valency of boron is? At least is French tomorrow. That is easy and useful.

Friday 15

I take it back. French was utterly impossible and did not involve the words '*superbe*' or '*zut alors*' at all. Do not know why we learn the language anyway. No one speaks it except the French, who are economically irrelevant, and Celine Dion. We should be learning Japanese so that we can all run IT conglomerates. And purchase ironic knee-length socks on our travels.

Saturday 16

Hurrah. Glastonbury tickets have arrived. Jack gave me mine at work. It is marked 'sex—male'. And claims I am

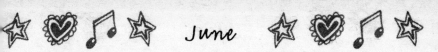
thirty-five. It is an understandable mistake. After all have used excellent nickname Ray. Plus do actually look bit like boy. Told Jack I still hadn't managed to persuade Mum to let me go. Or even mention it to her in fact. He said I could tell her we are all going to visit Granny Stone in Jersey for healthy post-GCSE recovery featuring bicycle riding and horses. He says he will happily lie for me, as Mum will not believe Suzy. Was so pleased forgot to dig for head boy battle dirt. Will make something up to Justin later.

9 p.m.
Mum has agreed to let me go to Jersey on the proviso that I do not go near the indigenous criminal fraternity. She is *Bergerac*-obsessed and thinks all the millionaires are diamond-smuggling lotharios or drug dealers. It is lucky she has never met Granny Stone. According to Scarlet she smokes marijuana. I said it is practically legal if it is for arthritis purposes. She said it is not. It is for getting high purposes.

Sunday 17
Father's Day

Revision interrupted for day due to arrival of Jesus and Grandpa for multi-generational Father's Day celebration. Mum pointed out that they had not been invited but Grandpa said Treena was sick of them getting under her feet. Mum said why, is she doing the hoovering for once?

Grandpa said no. It is one of Mrs O'Grady's get fit DVDs. Treena is wasting her time if Mrs O'Grady is anything to go by. She is gargantuan. On plus side they acted as a distraction from fact that I had utterly forgotten Father's Day. Dad said not to worry as passing my GCSEs will be a present in itself. Wish had got him golf balls now. He is going to be doubly cross if I fail.

Monday 18

Oh my God. Have just had Geography exam. Did not even remember I was doing Geography and omitted it entirely from revision schedule. It is lucky I sat exam at all and is only down to Scarlet texting me to ask me where I was and what was the capital of Bulgaria. Will do better than Emily Reeve anyway. She had to go to the toilet ten times in two hours. (According to Mark Lambert it is because the baby is sitting right on her bladder. Asked him how he knows. He says Mrs Duddy has been teaching them about babies, 'which are, like, the meaning of life'. Did not get into repeat of sex versus exams versus 42 argument. And admire Mrs Duddy for teaching the Retards and Criminals something they will actually need to know, as opposed to raffia owls and *Olga da Polga*.) Fat Kylie also went to the loo several times. She is not pregnant. She had got a packet of Jaffa cakes stashed on top of the cistern.

Have got History tomorrow. Will do Cold War questions

as am excellent on that e.g. *Pravda* is not a fashion brand, is an evil Russian *Daily Mail*-type paper. And iron curtain is not in Poland.

Tuesday 19

But should probably have found out what *perestroika* and *glasnost* were. Oh well. It is too late now. Only Rural Studies to go and no one has ever failed that.

5 p.m.
Except Stacey O'Grady. And that was only because he was in custody for kidnapping a police Alsatian on the day of the exam. (The police should be the ones in trouble. The Alsatian put up no resistance and broke several codes by accepting sweets from strangers and getting into their car.)

Wednesday 20

Do not remember ducks being on syllabus. Or maybe we were all watching Mark Lambert do the Macarena at the time instead of concentrating on the interactive whiteboard.

Anyway it will be declared null and void because Emily Reeve went into labour in the middle of the exam. Fat Kylie shrieked, 'Sir, Emily's pissed herself, sir.' Mark Lambert, with his newly discovered obstetrician skills, said, 'No she

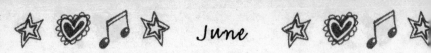

ain't, you fat idiot, her waters have broke, innit.' And he ushered her to Mrs Leech for bourbons and a sanitary towel. Everyone is on tenterhooks now waiting for news. Mark, Emily's self-appointed midwife, has gone in the ambulance and is going to text with news. He is hoping it is a boy so it can be named in his honour. The rest of us have decamped to the Common with several bottles of cider to celebrate the end of exams.

4 p.m.
Text from Mark. Emily is five centimetres dilated. What is dilated? Thought only eyeballs got dilated on drugs. Maybe it is the gas and air. Though five centimetre-wide eyeballs would be a bit excessive and mental looking.

5 p.m.
Text from Mark. He has seen Emily's hoo-ha. And it is hairier than Thin Kylie's.

5.30 p.m.
Text from Mark saying this will be his last text as phone is being confiscated by fat mardy woman. He means Mrs Reeve.

11 p.m.
Emily Reeve has got a baby girl. Mark says she is named after him. Have texted to say cannot have girl called Mark.

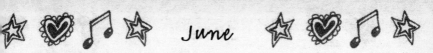

11.40 p.m.

He says baby is called Lola Lambert Reeve and is totally ginger. He has sent a photo of him holding her. She looks kind of content. Even in the perilous grip of a criminal. Thin Kylie is excited. She thinks he will get broody now and 'knock her up' so she can have one too.

11.45 p.m.

The Maths Club have narrowed the field for potential father down to Danny 'Duracell' Carrick in Year Eleven, 'Ginger' Rogers in Year Nine, and Mr Whippy, who has orangey stubble.

11.50 p.m.

Maths Club have ruled Mr Whippy out of running after Fat Kylie threatened to sit on them. She says there is no way Mr Whippy would stick his 99 in anyone that 'minging'.

Scarlet says it is very deep and meaningful (though is not 'meaning of life' per se, that is still sex) that a new life was born into Year Eleven just as we were all finishing our GCSEs and symbolically ending our childhoods etc. Except for people doing GCSE Needlework who have got a tapestry practical to go next week.

12.15 a.m.

Oh, and people doing AS PE who have got a keepy-uppy test on Tuesday i.e. Justin, which is why he says he did

not want to come out and celebrate in case it jeopardized his technique. (He is so dedicated.) Anyway, can sleep peacefully now, imbued with knowledge that have nothing to worry about any more.

1 a.m.
Oh God. Am going to Glastonbury tomorrow and have not even begun to plan wardrobe.

Thursday 21

Mum and Dad have given me a present for finishing my GCSEs. It is a digital camera. Mum says I can use it in Jersey to record my post-exam health-giving holiday. Presents from Mum are never straightforward. It is like when she finally got me a mobile phone so that she could check where I was at all times. This is just a further test to catch me out lying. Will just take photos of us looking rosy-cheeked against grassy backdrop. Glastonbury is bound to have loads of those. Have packed essential camping clothing i.e. miniskirt, flip-flops, lacy vest thingy, gigantic fluffy one-armed jumper, and sheepskin boot things (in case of inclement weather). Am ignoring Scarlet's warnings to bring waterproof clothing. There is no way I am wearing a cagoule, not even in a hurricane. I will just look like Mum. Plus my wellies are not uber-trendy pink Hunters. They are red Millets ones. Will just shelter in dance tent or something instead. Bob is picking me up in

the sick-smelling Volvo at eleven, to give us plenty of time
to find a good camping spot and pitch tents before dark.
Hurrah, am so excited. It is first foray into alternative drug
culture. By this time tomorrow will be holding heroin for A
list rock star while he waits in the queue for the Portaloo.

12 noon
Am here. But only just. Queue to get near Worthy Farm was
stretching back to the Taunton turn-off. Had to sit for five
hours on the M5 wedged in Jack's armpit. Then had panic
attack about not being allowed in due to ticket claiming I
am a thirty-five-year-old man called Ray. Suzy offered to
swap as she has no fear about lying to authority, but decided
I am more convincing as middle-aged man than busty sex
guru. Either security is lax or I really do look like Robert
Plant as the white rasta in the fluorescent vest who was
checking tickets waved me through with a nod of his blond
dreadlocks. Probably he is on drugs already. It is compulsory
to take several while you are here. I am aiming for cider and
herbal tea.

Anyway, am still too close to Jack's armpit for comfort
now due to Tony and Gordon having sprayed his one-
man dome (they are not spayed, Suzy says it is an affront
to their masculinity) and the smell being unbearable. We
are now having to share the storage pod in Scarlet's tent.
Jack refused to bed down with Bob and Suzy in case they
got tantric urges in the night. Have made a barrier from
food supplies (crisps, biscuits, chocolate brioche rolls) down

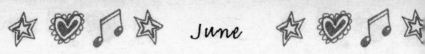
the middle in case he gets tantric urges and forgets I am not Sophie. Though one look at my 32As will remind him otherwise. Also it is raining and sheepskin boots are already soggy. Am hoping they will dry inside tent but humidity is currently at eighty per cent due to four sweaty teenagers in airtight nylon. Though on plus side am not cold. Am going now as Jack has told me to turn off Tweenies torch and stop rustling. It is not me. It is the Doritos.

Friday 22

8 a.m.
Have had no sleep due to constant crap samba drumming from two tents down and constant crap rain drumming on roof. Also the temperature dropped to Arctic conditions in the night and there is actual frost on the sheepskin boots.

9 a.m.
Trevor and Scarlet have gone out for day already in their waterproof gothwear. (Black wellies and poncho capes, which they claim are like bat outfits. They are not, they are like ponchos, which went out of fashion years ago after Catherine Zeta Jones started wearing them.) They asked if I wanted to join them on their journey of discovery (they are going to the Lost Vagueness field with Bob and Suzy, which is for hardcore mentalists and ageing hippies only).

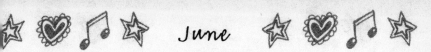
Declined due to footwear issues. Will try to heat boots up on Calor Gas stove to thaw them out.

10 a.m.
Have scorched hole in sheepskin boots. Jack says it only adds to their interesting look. He is just trying to make me feel better. They look crap. Am going to wear flip-flops.

12 noon
Have lost flip-flops in boggy patch on way to toilet queue. Am going to have to purchase wellies from Millets stall. Oh the irony. Jack says he will piggyback me there to save me getting even muddier. Have accepted. Am desperate.

3 p.m.
Have purchased new red wellies at extortionate price of £25 plus cagoule for £30. (Have accepted will have to look like Mum as all clothes now soggy. But will wear it with miniskirt as opposed to M&S elasticated waist beige linen.) Jack has lent me the money. Am so far in debt now, another £55 will not matter. He is being very nice. He carried me through the muddy hordes and only dropped me twice. Once when he tripped over a two year old in a tiger print leotard and once when we saw Richard Hammond in the toilet queue. Have texted Scarlet to see if she is coming back to the tent but she says she is busy having her crystals read.

5 p.m.

We are going to play I-spy in tent for now as it is too wet to go out and the queue for food poisoning noodles is right around the circus field.

8 p.m.

Have played 'I-spy', 'animal, vegetable, or mineral' and 'who'd you rather' (e.g. Mr Wilmott or Barry the Blade—answer Mr Wilmott, on hygiene grounds) for four hours and eaten entire supply of Doritos and Yoyos. Jack suggested we borrow Suzy's VIP pass and watch some celebrities fall out of their Winnebagos but is still raining and tent is warm again from hot Dorito breath. We are going to open a bottle of Strongbow instead and play more games.

1 a.m.

Have had very weird moment. It is not my fault. It is Jack's. Or possibly the man who invented Strongbow. Anyway, we didn't even go to the main stage because it was too far and anyway we can hear the bands from inside the tent which is almost the same as being there only without 125,000 people stamping on your feet or spilling warm beer on your head. But Jack said he was bored with 'parlour games' and suggested we played Truth or Dare. Which is usually fun because he used to dare me to jump off the shed roof or watch Eamonn Holmes for ten minutes without getting itchy and screaming. Only this time was kind of different. Jack picked Truth so I asked him why he was going out with Sophie. He

said, 'Because she has 34C breasts.' Then my face must have gone funny because he said, 'Joke, Riley. I don't know why. Because she was there. And she's not complicated.'

Then he asked me why I was going out with Justin. And I thought about it. Because there must be a hundred reasons. Like his good hair. And that he can play 'Stairway to Heaven' on guitar. But none of them sounded enough. Then I remembered the stuff about trust. So I said, 'Because he tells me everything.' And then I told him about Kelly's pants to prove the point. Jack said, 'You're wrong, you know.' I said, 'No. He told me. It was in Year Ten.' Jack said, 'Not about that.' So I said, 'Fine, your turn.'

Then he looked at me for what felt like a really long time, but I know for a fact was only a few seconds because I was actually counting in my head for some reason, and then he said 'Dare'. And then, and I don't know why, because *a*) I am going out with Justin and *b*) it is a total Truth or Dare cliché, I dared him to kiss me. But at that moment it didn't sound bad, or like a cliché. It sounded like a good idea. And he must have thought so too, because he did. And it was like that moment in *Bugsy Malone* again when I tried to think about Aunty Joyless but I still felt funny inside. And I realized that it never feels like that with Justin. Not once. But then my phone rang and it was Scarlet to say that she and Trevor were sleeping in a tepee with some Aztecs and a man called Horse so I could move pod if I wanted. But, even though the moment was gone, I didn't want to move. And nor did Jack. So we are now lying next to each other listening to someone playing Kaiser Chiefs really badly

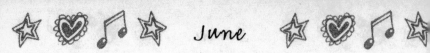

on a banjo. But the Doritos barrier is gone because we ate it. And I am not sure what is going to happen next. And I am not sure what I want to happen next.

1.05 a.m.
Jack just told me to stop writing because he is trying to sleep and my elbow is digging him in the ribs every time I finish a line. Which is an answer I guess.

Saturday 23

11 a.m.
Things are back to normal with Jack i.e. we are not speaking again. Woke up with my head on Jack's arm. Said, 'Sorry.' He said, 'It doesn't hurt.' I said, 'I didn't mean that. I meant last night.' So he said, 'I'm sorry too.' Then I said, 'It didn't mean anything.' Because that is what you are supposed to say—I have seen it in a million films and then he says, 'But it did to me,' etc., etc. But Jack obviously has not seen these films because he said, 'Too right.' So I said, 'Totally. Because I am in love with Justin.' So then Jack said, 'Has he called you?' So I said, 'No. But it is because there is no signal between here and Saffron Walden. Or else he is busy on his head boy campaign.' Jack just said, 'Whatever you want to believe.'

And then before I could say anything witty Scarlet and Trevor arrived back from the Aztec tepee. She said the man called Horse sang Dolly Parton songs all night and they have

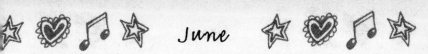

had no sleep so they have bought herbal sleeping pills off a man with a helmet shaped like an eel and are going to bed for the day. Which they did.

Then Jack said, 'Scarlet is mental. Those tablets could be anything.'

So for some reason I said, 'I think I might take one, actually, as I have had not very much sleep (which is true, due to wondering what Jack would do in the night: answer nothing, as he can clearly sleep through several drunk Brummies playing bongos on a saucepan and singing 'Every day I love you less and less') and I want to feel refreshed for tonight.'

Jack said, 'Don't, Riley. You don't have to prove anything to me.'

I said, 'I'm not doing it for you. I'm doing it for me.' And then I swallowed it with some warm Tizer. But it is obviously a fake as do not feel any differ—

Sunday 24

9 p.m.

Oh God. Have somehow lost entire day. Thought had woken up at five after several hours of refreshing sleep but actually have been asleep for thirty-two hours and need to wee really badly. There is no sign of Trevor and Scarlet. They must be hardened to herbal drugs. Or maybe they woke up half an hour ago and have gone out to score some more. I can hear Jack outside though. He is on the phone

and is shouty. Do not want to see him as he is obviously in mood and bound to say 'I told you so' but have to pee. Will just do it in Pringles tube and empty it outside later. Will be like Bear Grylls or Ray Mears.

9.15 p.m.
Have peed in Pringles tube but cardboard is leaking slightly so have wrapped it in a plastic bag and put it at bottom of rucksack. Oh God, Jack is coming in.

11 p.m.
Jack did not say, 'I told you so.' He said, 'Did you know your moronic boyfriend is round Sophie's house?' I said, 'No, and he is not moronic he just looks like that when he is thinking hard but anyway it is obviously not Justin's fault it is because your idiotic girlfriend has lured him there with her big breasts and uncomplicatedness.'

Jack said, 'She's not my girlfriend any more.' So I said, 'Oh.' And then Jack just said, 'I'm going out.' Which he did. And now am all riled up and angry and not sure who at. It is probably Jack. He is a liar. Justin is not interested in Sophie. He is probably just there to commiserate with her that me and Jack are away. And Jack has jumped to conclusions. That is it. Will just text Justin to check though.

11.30 p.m.
No answer. And Jack is back. He says he has secured agreement from Suzy that we are leaving at 6 a.m. He has

erected a rucksack barrier in the pod and has gone to bed. Am not tired though so will sit up and gaze at stars through tent flap. And text Justin again.

11.45 p.m.
No answer. And Jack has told me to stop beeping because he cannot sleep. Although oddly the sound of Coke bottle and pasta maracas from two tents down does not appear to be disturbing him at all. Justin is obviously asleep. Will just wait until we are reunited tomorrow. Am still not tired though. Will go for walk to observe the dying hours of my first Glastonbury.

12.15 a.m.
Am back from walk due to too many bodies strewn over the paths. It is like scene from Hogarth's 'Gin Lane'. Also Tweenies torch ran out of batteries and tripped over a tent peg and skewered myself on wind chime so now probably have black eye to add to mud-drenched wild-haired look. Trevor and Scarlet are still not back. They are probably doing something with the druids.

4 a.m.
Still awake. As are several tents around me from which I can distinctly hear someone playing the theme to *Neighbours*. At least Scarlet and Trevor are back safely. They were not with the druids. They were helping Bob find Suzy who went missing in the Field of Lost Vagueness two days ago.

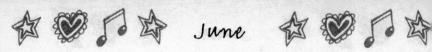
5 a.m.

Am asleep now. Will lie down next to Jack and the impenetrable rucksack barrier. Although sleeping bag feels a bit soggy. Maybe it is Jack's tears.

Monday 25

9 a.m.

Was not Jack's tears. Was Pringles wee. The tube had disintegrated and contents leaked out of anti-suicide airhole in Waitrose carrier bag. Plus had put it in Jack's rucksack by mistake and now his clothes are all wet. Told him it was apple juice. Think he believed me although he did question why I was storing apple juice in a Pringles tube. Am happy none the less. It is because he is wearing a wee-stained jumper. Whereas I am wee-free. It is retribution for lying about Justin. We are leaving as soon as Suzy wakes up. Which may be hours as it turns out she bought a herbal pill off the eel-helmet man last night.

11 p.m.

Am home. Bob got bored waiting for Suzy so he and Trevor just carried her to the sick-smelling Volvo. She is still asleep now. I envy her. She did not have to suffer a seven-hour wait on the M25 or Jack's silence treatment. Or his pervading smell of my wee (detectable even above lingering scent of

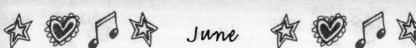
vomit). I said they could drop me at Justin's so we could be reunited in our love. Jack snorted. He is horrible and I hate him. Anyway Justin was in and not with Sophie so he is definitely a liar. I threw my arms around him in full view of the reversing Volvo and said did you miss me? He said, 'You kind of smell.' And shrank away. Checked when got home. He is right. I do smell. Plus am channelling Mrs Simpson look.

Mum was shocked by appearance. I said Jersey was tougher than I expected. With less soap. James said I should sue *Bergerac* for false advertising.

11.15 p.m.
Mum has just stuck head round door to say she is looking forward to viewing digital photos. Oh God. Will check them in morning. And have bath. Am too tired now from seminal Glastonbury experience. It is not exactly how I imagined. But on plus side have taken herbal drugs. And drunk cider. And weed in a Pringles tube. So am practically Amy Winehouse.

11.45 p.m.
Maybe could sell Pringles tube wee invention and make fortune. Though plastic not cardboard.

12 midnight
Maybe should go to bed now and stop Googling portable wee equipment.

Tuesday 26

A terrible thing has happened. The North of England and several bits near Wales have been flooded. Sheffield, Hull, and Gloucester are almost entirely submerged according to prone-to-exaggeration GMTV. James says they are like Nineveh city and is God's way of punishing the wicked. Mum agrees.

At least the floods have temporarily distracted everyone from lack of digital evidence of the so-called Jersey holiday. Thank God. I have checked the camera and have only got three photos. One of Jack grinning in front of a naked man on stilts (not very Jersey). One of Trevor and Scarlet eating Vegeburgers in the Green field (not very Jersey unless it has an indigenous midget-dressed-as-drag-queen population). And one of me in eel-helmet man herbal sleeping tablet coma. Am going to have to mock up shots. Or claim camera does not work.

Wednesday 27

Scarlet rang to invite me for high tea of hummus and breadsticks. Have declined as *a*) Jack will be there and *b*) I can't think of another reason but a) is good enough. Instead am going round Sad Ed's to get him to take photos of me looking rosy-cheeked and Enid Blytonesque. Have put on extra blusher to compensate for current post-Glastonbury pasty look.

3 p.m.

Sad Ed has taken four photos. They are all close-ups of me in his back garden. He said Mum would be able to forensically identify all other Saffron Walden landmarks if we did them in town. As it is he is worried she will be able to pinpoint the rhododendron to 24 Loompits Avenue.

Thursday 28

Showed Mum holiday photos at breakfast. She seemed satisfied. James asked why they were all taken yesterday at 2.45 p.m., according to the timer. But luckily Mum does not understand gadgetry (it is men's work) and told him to be quiet and eat his muesli. It is because he is in trouble at school again. Keanu is demanding that he takes the dog in so he can be their wolf protector in the playground. Mum says there is no way the dog is going near St Regina's, or Keanu for that matter, as it is a recipe for disaster, and anti-social behaviour. She is right. The dog makes Keanu look conscientious.

Friday 29

Hurrah. Am going round Justin's tonight for a snog. It will be our first since before Glastonbury due to me smelling too much on Monday night and him doing overtime mincing

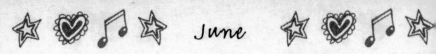
meat for Mr Goddard all week. Am going to refresh all orifices. Actually just one, i.e. clean teeth. And wear Lenor-scented clothes so do not risk rejection on odour grounds again. It will be an utterly earth-shattering moment.

9 p.m.

Was not earth-shattering. Was mediocre. And brief. In fact less than ten seconds. I was counting in head again (why do I do that?), using the infallible one elephant, two elephant method. He is still oddly distant despite me smelling lemon fresh. It is probably the head boy battle. Apparently he is lagging in the Maths Club polls.

10 p.m.

Or maybe he has found out about me kissing Jack in the Truth or Dare game at Glastonbury. Oh God. That may be it. Will interrogate Jack behind the lentil bins tomorrow.

Saturday 30

Jack claims he has said nothing about the snog. He said, 'Why in God's name would I want people to know I had kissed you, Riley? I'm not insane.' Which is possibly true. It does not explain Justin's behaviour though. And he has a gig tonight. The Back Doors are playing a rugby club disco at Henham Village Hall to which I am not invited as there is not enough room in the Transit van. I said I could get a lift in the Passat

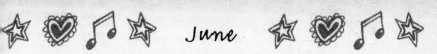

so I could do groupie duties but Justin said not to bother as he will be mobbed anyway. I pointed out that it is, in fact, our six month anniversary at about 11.59 tonight. He said we should wait and see if we have been going out a year and then celebrate. He is right. Six months is nothing when we have a lifetime ahead of us. And am probably worrying over nothing. This is just normal rock star behaviour. And wives do not go to all gigs, they stay at home eating macrobiotic food and doing yoga. May well try it. Though will watch *Casualty* first as trailer showed excellent helicopter crash.

I'm RACHEL RILEY

— welcome to my so-called life.

July

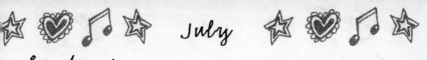

Sunday 1

School starts again tomorrow. It is Sixth Form induction i.e. hanging around looking louche and drinking black Nescafé.

Monday 2

I was right. Spent entire day drinking Nescafé and listening to crap mix CDs on ancient common room stereo. Am now feeling all shaky due to excess caffeine and thrash metal. May have to lie down. Sad Ed says it is the pinnacle of one's Sixth Form career to get control of the 'decks' for the day. He is delighted as he now has something to aim for in life. Thought Justin might grasp opportunity that am now officially allowed to sit on saggy sofa to try to snog me vigorously on it. But he is still distant. It is because he is struggling to win over the Marxist vote. They are favouring Jack who has a Lenin T-shirt. The head girl fight is already over. It will be Sophie Microwave Muffins. She has got the sympathy vote because Jack has chucked her. Also her only rival is Oona Rickets and she is bisexual and smelly. Not that they are related. It is just an observation. It is perfectly possibly to be gay and pleasant-scented.

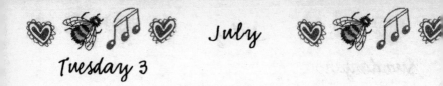
Sixth Form induction is utterly pointless. Mr Wilmott tried to make us do getting-to-know-each-other games where we all confess something secret about ourselves and abandon our old cliques and embrace difference. The silence was deafening until he left to sort out a locust escape in the mobile science labs and everyone got out their *Grazias* and iPods and carried on hanging out with the same people they have always hung out with.

On the plus side, the riddle of Lola Lambert Reeve's father has been solved. It is not Danny 'Duracell' Carrick or Ginger Rogers but someone called Brian from Didsbury. According to Thin Kylie who heard it off Fat Kylie who heard it off Emily's new best friend and baby guru Mark Lambert, they met on a scout and guide jamboree in the Lake District, which is proof that even the dullest of resorts are a risk to teenage pregnancy statistics. Mum will be annoyed. She has always pinpointed Butlins and Magalluf as chief culprits. In contrast, the Maths Club are jubilant as no one guessed right. They have made a record £87 from all the betting. Emily should have put some money on herself. Nappies are very expensive. I once caught Treena trying to dry one with her Remington volumizer so she could re-use it.

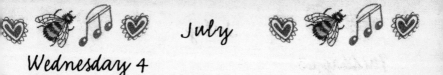
Wednesday 4

James has begun a campaign to have a sleepover party on Saturday. He wants to invite Mad Harry, Keanu, and Maggot. I said there is no chance. He said he does not expect to get all of them past Mum's stringent checks. He is aiming high and hoping for just Mad Harry. It is a brilliant plan.

Thursday 5

Mum still not agreeing to sleepover. James offered to drop Maggot from the guest list but she is still unmoved. He said he is not giving in as he still has his trump card to play. It is dropping Keanu.

Also Granny Clegg's hip has moved to the top of the waiting list. It is because someone called Mrs Bean has electrocuted herself on a can opener. Granny is scheduled for the chop at the end of July. Mum says she will go down to help out but Granny Clegg says there is no need because Grandpa Clegg is quite capable of heating up Fray Bentos. Mum says she is definitely going down then if Grandpa Clegg is in charge. He is notoriously crap at all things household.

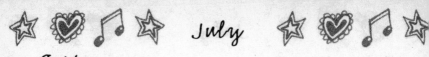
Friday 6

Mum has agreed to James's sleepover with Mad Harry following his cunning plan of dropping Keanu from the guest list. She was worried he might infect the bedding with his ringworm. As it is she made him sit on a rubber sheet at James's birthday party. James is jubilant. They are going to have Ninja rituals. Am going to absent self from house by going to Sad Ed's. Would go to Justin's but he is still too focused on his campaign to do any snogging. I pointed out that it is weeks since he has put his tongue in my mouth with any kind of conviction. He said it will all be different once the head boy results are in. I hope so.

Saturday 7

Sophie Microwave Muffins went into Goddard's three times today. What can she possibly want with all that meat? Unless she is planning a head girl celebratory barbecue party. Which is possible. Had to pretend was not interested though as Jack was watching me from behind the till of death. Mr Goldstein has posted him on it permanently as he has manly fingers, which do not bruise so easily.

Tuesday and Scarlet also at Sad Ed's. Scarlet was supposed to be in the bat cave (i.e. Trevor's goth shrine bedroom) but they have had a row. It is over the O'Grady liaison. She confessed to it during a heated sexual moment (Trevor was

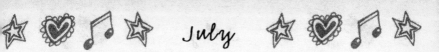
wafting his black hair over her legs at the time). Scarlet argued that they were 'on a break' but Trevor is not cross because of the infidelity as much as who it was with. It is because the O'Gradys are at the forefront of local anti-goth feeling i.e. they are constantly calling him Dracula.

Scarlet says we should make the prom an anti-prom and go together, but not as lezzers. Pointed out that I still had a date i.e. prospective head boy and rock god Justin Statham. But Tuesday said he will go with Sophie as it is ancient American prom custom. Sad Ed said this is Saffron Walden, not South Central. How right he is.

Sunday 8

8 a.m.
Have been rudely awakened, literally, by naked James and Mad Harry in Hallowe'en masks. It was terrifying. Thought was being attacked by murderous pygmy people and a wolf. They had persuaded the dog to take part in their nude antics. But more importantly, am having prom dress panic. It is less than a week to go to the most important night of my life and my only options are my fairy outfit from Grandpa Riley's wedding or the one from Uncle Jim's wedding with compost stains on it from where I tried to be Ophelia floating in the muddy river. Ooh. Maybe Mum will have a dress stashed in attic from the 1950s. Will be utter vintage prom queen. Hurrah!

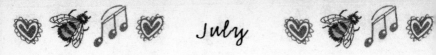

9 a.m.

Mum got all thin-lipped and said she was not born in the 1950s and all she has in the attic are some baby clothes, her wedding dress, and the mint-green jumpsuit with criminally tapered legs (she did not say that bit, she actually used the word 'nice'). She is not happy about the prom because it is American and she says the only good things to come out of America are potatoes and Ford cars. Asked to see the wedding dress. It is an eighties nightmare of nylon and lace. But it is at least knee length. Mum does not believe in long wedding dresses due to staining of hemline issues and wasting of material.

11 a.m.

Have had genius idea. Am going to butcher wedding dress, fairy outfit, and compost dress and create amazing new prom-style outfit. Will be totally like that bit in *Pretty in Pink*. Will even put bit of lace on dog to recreate the moment.

12 noon

Now have bedroom strewn with bits of bodice and the dog has eaten some of the pink fur off the fairy outfit. Will put bits in bag and take it all round to Sad Ed's. He did Needlework in Year Eight and knows how to do backstitch. Plus his mum has sewing machine as she used to make all of Ed's clothes. Have witnessed him in brown corduroy dungarees before. Which is bordering on child abuse.

4 p.m.

Have got new and fabulousish dress. It is quite vintage with a modern twist i.e. fairy wings and a tail. Have tried it on at home. James (now fully clothed) said I looked like something from Middle Earth. This is a compliment in his book. Mum says it is a shame I will never get to wear her wedding dress when I walk down the aisle. I said am not getting married as it is bourgeois convention and is only a bit of paper. Dad said, 'I wish someone had told me that,' but he said it too loud and Mum heard him and sent him to declog the gutters.

Monday 9

9 a.m.
Scarlet and Trevor are back together.

10 a.m.
Scarlet and Trevor have broken up again. Scarlet says this time it is for good though. She is sick of his controlling ways. And he has possible erectile issues. Which is too much information. They will be back together within days, if not minutes, anyway. She cannot resist his pale weedy charms.

12 noon
Oh God. Evil and unsubstantiated rumours are circulating John Major High about Justin's potential gayness. Ali Hassan

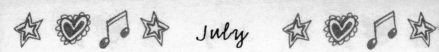

(aka head mathlete) asked me if it is true he wears women's underwear. Think have quashed them though by explaining mitigating circumstances i.e. his were all filthy at time.

Tuesday 10

Rumour situation worse. There are now rumours that the original rumours have been substantiated by an unnamed source close to Justin. Will deny everything. That is what Suzy does and she is an esteemed Labour councillor.

3 p.m.

Justin has hauled me into his campaign headquarters (aka the Sixth Form kitchen aka leaky microwave corner) to grill me about the pants rumour. I said it wasn't me it was Jack. Then he said how did Jack know and I said I may have let it out by mistake at Glastonbury but was under influence of cider at the time so was mentally diminished (the O'Gradys are always using this excuse in court) and was only telling him anyway as example of how much we trust each other etc. He said, 'You have broken that trust irredeemably.' Was momentarily shocked by his use of five syllable word during which time he stalked off. Possibly to repair damage done by Jack's evil rumour. It will all be OK though. He will forgive me when he realizes I did it out of love. And when I let him do 'It' on Friday. Suzy says sex is the best way to heal an argument.

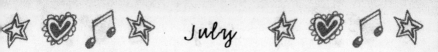
4 p.m.
Have texted Jack. THANKS FOR RUINING MY LIFE. It is almost true.

4.15 p.m.
Jack has texted back. NOT ME. WOULD NEVER HURT YOU.
Am ignoring it. He is a compulsive liar.

Wednesday 11

Justin is still not speaking to me. He is too busy trying to salvage his campaign in the dying hours (voting is tomorrow morning). He is wearing visible boxer shorts (Marks & Spencer) to confirm his masculinity. Just the sight of them makes me want him more. Or maybe it is because he is playing it cool. It is the oldest trick in the book, according to Scarlet. I asked her if Trevor is still playing it cool. She said arctic, but she is not falling for it again.

Also, disaster has struck Sad Ed. Mike Wandering Hands's wandering hands have wandered again. Edie caught him in a passionate clinch with his latest victim in a layby near Newport. I asked how. He said she still has stalking issues. Anyway, Edie is leaving after all and taking Tuesday with her. They are flying out on Sunday. On the plus side it means she will still be able to be Sad Ed's date

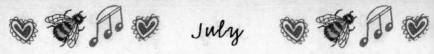

for the prom. Though he is going to have to spend most of his time scanning the upper school canteen for potential replacements.

Thursday 12

It is election day. Have texted Justin good luck but no reply as yet. He is probably using phone to talk last minute tactics with his team. Just had thought. Why am I not on team? Am excellent political co-ordinator, as proven by my role in Jack's successful election as Prime Minister of John Major High (role abandoned due to lack of any discernible powers). Maybe that is why. He thinks I am secretly loyal to Jack. He is wrong. I do not care about Jack at all. He is nothing to me.

11 a.m.

Have voted. For Justin, obviously. And for Oona Rickets, despite her smell and lesbian manifesto. At least she has average sized breasts. Scarlet is an utter traitor and has voted for Jack. It is because he has promised to instigate a goth tolerance day. Sad Ed says he is reserving the right not to reveal his political colours. He will have voted for Jack as well. He is hoping to take Tuesday's place as lead singer in the Jack Stone Five. He has no chance. He cannot even hold 'Frère Jacques' without going flat. Exit polls are putting Jack and Justin neck and neck. It may come down

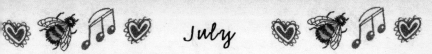
to Mr Wilmott's deciding vote. He has Simon Cowell-like jurisdiction in these matters.

3 p.m.

Jack has won the election by three votes. But it is a hollow victory. It is because Laurie Walsh (who once had a trial for Tottenham youth) dropped out of the race with suspected groin strain and all his supporters (ten of them) voted for Jack because he once went to White Hart Lane when he was eight. On the plus side, Sophie Microwave Muffins Jacobs is NOT head girl. It is smelly Oona. Voting was neck and neck so Mr Wilmott got the deciding vote and went for the underdog. It is not because he thinks she is better. It is to avoid accusations of anti-lesbianism and possible protest action.

Also, it turns out Oona encouraged her gay and lesbian alliance voters to support knicker-wearing Justin. So my pants rumour may actually have helped him in the end despite ultimate failure. Tried to tell him this and give him a commiseratory hug but he was too busy trying to revive Sophie Microwave Muffins who was sobbing all over the saggy sofa. Oh God. This is all wrong. I should be ensconced in a position of power, not watching my boyfriend whispering stuff to someone with discernible breasts and who does 'It', i.e. not me.

There is no other way forward. Cannot compete on breast front so will have to outdo Sophie on doing 'It' grounds. Am going round to seek advice from Suzy immediately and will astound him with my sexual prowess at the prom.

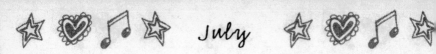

7 p.m.

Am now sex genius. There is nothing I do not know. Except things that are illegal or hurt, which I said I did not want to learn about as may have bad dreams. Also have assorted pack of condoms as do not want to end up like Emily Reeve, who I saw on way home with her mum and Lola Lambert. She has bleeding nipples. (Emily. Not her mum. Or Lola Lambert.) Scarlet says I should not do anything unless I am absolutely sure he is the ONE and she is glad she fended off Trevor now that he is not hers; in fact, her reluctance was probably a sign that he was all wrong. I said, *au contraire*, I am utterly sure, and non-reluctant (luctant?). Plus if I don't then I am definitely not going to be his ONE for any longer.

When I left Jack ran down the block paving and cornered me behind the sick-smelling Volvo. He said, 'Don't do it. He's not worth it.' I said, 'He's worth a million of you.' Which is actually from *Our Mutual Friend* but sounded excellently dramatic and made Jack go very quiet. Then he said, 'Just so you know, it wasn't me who spread the pants rumours, it was Sophie.' I said, 'Why would she do that if she likes Justin so much?' He said, 'To get you in trouble.' And then I couldn't think of anything clever to say so I just said, 'Bog off, Jack,' and left before he could have the last word.

He is wrong about me and Justin. And will show him tomorrow when we are totally the King and Queen of the John Major High prom.

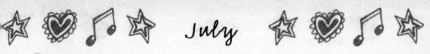

Friday 13

11 a.m.
Am above worrying about Friday 13th Twilight Zone issues. Nothing can go wrong. Tonight is the most important night of life so far as in approximately twelve hours will be losing virginity. Not sure exactly where yet but as long as it is not round the back of Goddard's or in the lower school toilets does not matter as will be swept away on emotion, not admiring surroundings.

Also it is Mum's birthday. Have given her an electric fly swat. She has been coveting one for ages to add to her anti-vermin arsenal.

3 p.m.
Electric fly swat declared a success. Has already despatched three bluebottles and stunned the dog into silence when it got caught in crossfire.

5 p.m.
Am getting dressed then can practise looking confident in haute couture prom dress. Scarlet has texted to see if I want to meet round hers then Bob can take us all in the Volvo. She says there is no shame in going to the prom alone. On the contrary it is utterly feminist and modern. I said I was old-fashioned and would be waiting for my date to pick me up in a limousine, or at least a pine-scented Viceroy taxi.

6 p.m.
Grandpa has been round to see me in prom dress. Actually he brought Jesus round for tea as their microwave is on the blink but he was very excited about it all none the less. He said I reminded him of a young Grandma Riley. James said she had varicose veins and kept bees. He said, 'Yes, that's it, the bees.' It must be my ironic veil. Or maybe the wings.

7 p.m.
Can see Thin Kylie out of the window in her 'prom dress' i.e. a tube of gold Lycra with bits cut out in the middle. She is getting a lift on Mr Hosepipe's fire engine. It is very romantic. But not as romantic as my carriage will be when it gets here. Oooh. Maybe it is an actual carriage with horses.

7.10 p.m.
No sign of Justin. Mum has stuck her head round door to ask what time he is coming exactly as she and Dad want to pop over to Marjory's and could I watch James for half an hour. Realized I hadn't checked. In fact, realized he has never officially asked me to prom at all. But he does not need to. He is my boyfriend so it is unwritten. Said he will be here by 7.30. Am sure of it.

7.45 p.m.
Still no sign of Justin. Dad has offered to run me to the school in the Passat. Have declined. It would be too humiliating. He might try to dance.

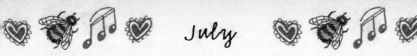
7.50 p.m.

Oooh. Doorbell. This must be him. Hurrah. Have condom (pineapple flavour, on loan from Sad Ed) stashed in special hidden pocket (fashioned by Sad Ed for this purpose exactly) and orifices are all clean (and not just teeth this time—have borrowed Suzy's 'feminine deodorant').

8 p.m.

It wasn't Justin. It was Jack. I said, 'What are you doing here?' He said, 'I've come to take you to the prom. I'm your emergency back-up man. Like Ross, when Rachel is stood up. Or Duckie in *Pretty in Pink*.' And I must admit, in his tuxedo and Converse he did look kind of cool, and Duckie-like. But that is not the point so I said, 'Duh, Ross never took Rachel to the prom. I don't need an emergency back-up man because I have a first-choice one and he will be here any minute to explore the meaning of life with me so I would go if I were you.' He said, 'He's not coming. He's gone with Sophie. They've been seeing each other for months. That's why we broke up.'

And then I felt a bit sick, like when Dad drives over humpback bridges too quickly just to make James scream, and had to sit down. And Jack said, 'Come on, Riley. That dress deserves to be seen. So you can either stay at home and kid yourself, or you can show the world, or at least John Major High, that he didn't break you.' Which was possibly the nicest thing anyone has ever said to me. Except then I remembered that it is from *Pretty in Pink* as well and was

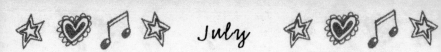

probably just another one of his lies to get at Justin and that I hate him. So I said, 'Just bugger off, will you. Don't you have head boy duties to do?'

And then he stood up and sighed in the way that James does when he knows I have got the answer wrong on *Eggheads* and said, 'Fine. But, Riley, sex isn't the meaning of life.' So I said, 'Really, so what is then, Einstein?' He said, 'Love.' And then he went because Bob was beeping the Volvo horn madly.

Anyway, he is wrong. About the meaning of life. And about Justin. He will show up. Any minute. I just know it.

Won't he?

Joanna Nadin grew up in the small, and tragically normal town of Saffron Walden in Essex. In a bid to make her life more like it is in books, she went to university to study Drama and become a famous actress. Instead, she somehow ended up as a Special Adviser to the Prime Minister. The Rachel Riley books are based entirely on these failed formative years, and her own peculiar family (she sends apologies to James for not even bothering to change his name).

As well as this bestselling series, Joanna has written numerous award-winning books for younger readers, has been shortlisted for the Roald Dahl Funny Prize, and thrice shortlisted for Queen of Teen. She now lives in Bath with her daughter Millie.

How it all started . . .

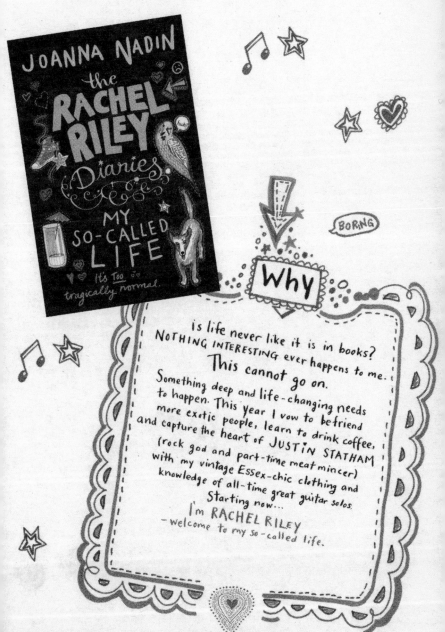

JOANNA NADIN

the
RACHEL
RILEY
Diaries

MY
SO-CALLED
LIFE

It's TOO
tragically normal.

BORING

Why

is life never like it is in books?
NOTHING INTERESTING ever happens to me.
This cannot go on.
Something deep and life-changing needs
to happen. This year I vow to befriend
more exotic people, learn to drink coffee,
and capture the heart of JUSTIN STATHAM
(rock god and part-time meat mincer)
with my vintage Essex-chic clothing and
knowledge of all-time great guitar solos.
Starting now...
I'm RACHEL RILEY
— welcome to my so-called life.

And how it carries on . . .

JOANNA NADIN

the RACHEL RILEY Diaries

MY (NOT SO) SIMPLE LIFE

No boys allowed...

Dumped!

I cannot believe it.
Am racked by torture and loss!
Have wanted tragedy in my life for
so long but now I've got it, it actually
sort of sucks... big time!

Have made a plan to deal with post break-up
trauma i.e. will not moon about over exes
but will embrace single life. Everything will
be so much easier and I am fully committed.
Starting now! Or at least, after breakfast...

RACHEL RILEY
—welcome to my so-called life.

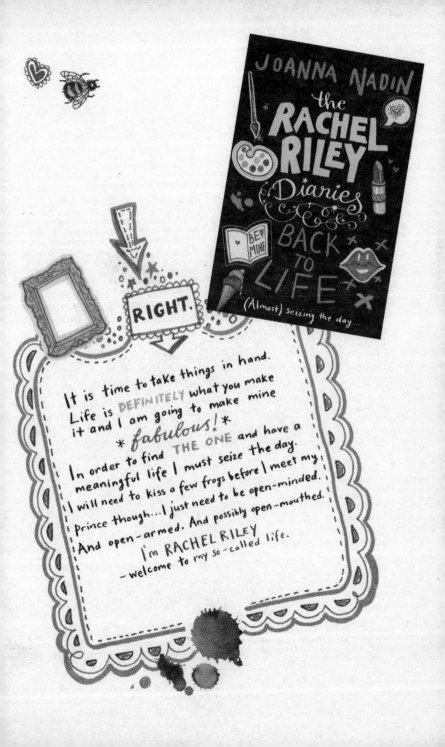